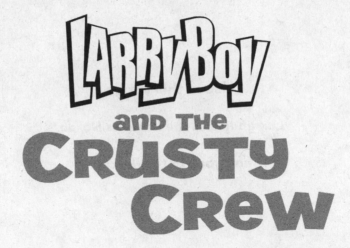

LarryBoy
and the
CRUSTY CREW

Also in this series

Larryboy and the Hideous Horde

Larryboy to the Rescue

ZONDERKIDZ
www.zonderkidz.com

Larryboy and the Crusty Crew
ISBN 978-0310-73857-2

Larryboy in the Attack of Outback Jack © 2003
Larryboy and the Yodelnapper © 2003
Larryboy in the Good, the Bad, and the Eggly © 2003

This title is also available as a Zondervan ebook.
Visit www.zondervan.com/ebooks

Requests for information should be addressed to:

Zonderkidz, 5300 Patterson Ave. SE, Grand Rapids, Michigan 49530

Larryboy and the Yodelnapper and *Larryboy in the Good, the Bad, and the Eggly* written by
Kent Reddecker
Larryboy and the Attack of Outback Jack written by Doug Peterson

Cover and Interior Illustrations: Michael Moore
Cover design and art direction: Big Idea Design, Paul Conrad, and Karen Poth
Interior design: Big Idea Design, Holli Leegwater, John Trent, and Karen Poth

Printed in the United States

13 14 15 16 17 18 19 20 21/DCI/ 15 14 13 12 11 10 9 8 7 6 5 4 3 2 1

3 books in 1

VeggieTales

LarryBoy
and the
CRUSTY
CREW

Kent Redeker & Doug Peterson

ZONDER**kidz**

VeggieTales®

LARRYBOY™

IN THE ATTACK OF OUTBACK JACK

WRITTEN BY
DOUG PETERSON

ILLUSTRATED BY
MICHAEL MOORE

BASED ON THE HIT VIDEO SERIES: LARRYBOY
CREATED BY PHIL VISCHER
SERIES ADAPTED BY TOM BANCROFT

ZONDERkidz

ZONDERVAN.com/
AUTHORTRACKER
follow your favorite authors

TABLE OF CONTENTS

CHAPTER 1

THEY CAME FROM THE SEA

It started with screams.

Lots of screaming. Then the swimmers at Bumbly Bay Beach started running, scrambling for shore.

Was it a shark attack? A monster? A deranged beach ball? Mutant lifeguards running in slow motion?

No! It was worse. Much worse.

It was a kiwi fruit.

A crazed kiwi was driving his jeep right across Bumbly Bay like a motorboat. The amphibious jeep sliced through the water, scattering swimmers, and then roared out onto the beach, swerving wildly to avoid sunbathers.

Behind the wheel was none other than that dastardly driver, Outback Jack. And in the seat next to him was his evil sidekick, Jackie, who was busily reading a best-selling book, *The Doofus' Guide to Treasure Hunting*.

"Oy, love! We made it!" boomed Outback Jack, who was as much Australian as kangaroos and crocodiles. He wore a khaki shirt and bush hat and talked with the gleeful excitement of a little kid.

"G'day, Bumblyburg!" Outback Jack shouted, as the jeep veered onto a street. "Outback Jack's the name, and fortune hunting's me game!" Throwing his head back, he roared with laughter.

"Hmmmm—that's the last time I let you drive us across the ocean," said Outback Jack's evil sidekick from behind her book. "Look what it's done to my hair!"

She lowered her book, revealing the most sinister sidekick in the long history of sinister sidekicks. She was hideous. She was shocking. She was...

A sock puppet?

Yes, it's true. Outback Jack's sidekick was none other than Jackie, the Sock Puppet. But she wasn't just any old sock puppet plucked warm from the dryer. She looked like a crocodile with a pink pillbox hat.

Outback Jack had a very special relationship with the sock puppet perched on his right hand. He spoke to her, and she spoke back. (But truth be told, Outback did all of Jackie's talking for her, speaking in a very high-pitched voice.)

This kiwi had clearly spent too much time alone in the outback.

"We're going to be the richest blokes in the world once we steal the legendary Treasure of Bumblyburg," grinned Outback, as he made a sharp right turn and nearly ran over two gourds.

"We'll show 'em, Jack," said the puppet. "We're going to steal the treasure, and then we'll... **AHHHHHHHHHHHHH!**"

The crocodile sock puppet stared straight ahead, open-mouthed with terror. The jeep was about to plow over Ma Mushroom. The little old lady had stepped off the curb and right into traffic, while casually licking her three-scoop ice cream cone.

SCREEEEEEEECHHH!

Outback Jack slammed on the brakes just in time. The jeep came to a skidding, squealing stop—inches before flattening Ma Mushroom.

Outback Jack couldn't help but stare at Ma Mushroom as the little old lady strolled in front of him, still licking her ice cream. In an excited whisper, he said, "Blimey! It's a flat-out Granny Crossing!"

Outback Jack crawled onto the hood of the jeep for a closer look. "Look how slow she moves," he gawked. "This is incredible! I've never seen a granny up close like this. They must be a very endangered species."

"Um...pardon us," Jackie the Sock Puppet crooned to Ma Mushroom in the sweetest tone. Then, in a voice that could shatter rock, she added, *But could you please move it, sister!*"

Jackie's yell was so loud that the force lifted Ma Mushroom off her feet and blew her backward. Her ice cream cone flew out of her hand and landed on the head of a cucumber standing on the corner. As for Ma Mushroom, she landed upside down in a nearby trashcan.

"'At's tellin' the old toadstool, Jackie!" laughed Outback Jack. Then he put the jeep in gear and tore off, leaving the smell of burned rubber hanging in the air.

"Whippersnapper!" Ma Mushroom called after him from inside the can.

Meanwhile, the cucumber on whose head the cone had landed, paused to lick the ice cream streaming down his face. "My favorite flavor—vanilla cheese crunch!"

Yes, you guessed it! That cucumber was none other than Larry the Cucumber, and standing beside him was his trusted manservant, Archibald. (Larry calls him "Archie" for short.)

"I don't like the looks of this, Master Lawrence," said Archie.

"You're right. Vanilla cheese crunch stains easily," said Larry. "Do you think you can get it out of my shirt?"

"No, I mean that crazy kiwi," Archie clarified. "I think

14

he's up to no good."

"Oh, right. That too," Larry agreed as he tossed aside the ice cream cone. "This looks like a job for Larryboy!"

Larry whistled for a taxi, which came screeching to the curb. He flung open the door and leaped inside. With tires spinning like an Indy 500 racecar, the taxi sped ahead for…well…just about three feet. Then it came to another screeching halt, and the back door sprang open again.

Out leaped the caped cucumber. The defender of vic-timized vegetables. The purple, plunger-headed protector of…

"We get the point," urged Archie.

It was Larryboy!

"I AM THAT HERO!" Larryboy shouted as he hopped off in hot pursuit of Outback Jack.

CHAPTER 2
THE KING OF CHAOS

Wherever Outback Jack went, chaos followed, and pandemonium was about to descend on Bumblyburg.

Outback drove his jeep straight to the offices of the *Daily Bumble* newspaper—and I do mean *straight*. If there was a building in his path, he drove right through it, scattering shoppers, pulverizing mannequins, and wreaking havoc along the way.

As the crazy kiwi and his sock puppet pulled up to the newspaper building, Outback hopped onto his jet-powered, boomerang-shaped glider. Riding the boomerang like a flying skateboard, he soared right through the open window of Bob the Tomato's office on the top floor.

"WHAAAAA...?" said Bob, diving for cover.

With madcap glee, Outback Jack began to tear apart the offices of the *Daily Bumble* and made a monstrous mess as he hunted for information about the infamous Treasure of Bumblyburg.

"Hey! You can't do

that!" shouted Bob, the newspaper editor.

"Try to stop me, tomato-face!"

Rifling through Bob's file cabinet, Outback Jack flung papers in the air. Bob scurried around trying to catch them as they rained down upon his office.

But Larryboy was right behind him!

Our superhero had used his fruit-seeking radar to track the crazed kiwi right to Bob's office—although all he had to do was follow the trail of destruction. He raced through the door and skidded to a halt as he struck a heroic pose.

"Halt, you evil ice-cream-cone-wrecking, file-snatchers!" Larryboy announced.

"I'll handle this," whispered Jackie into Outback's ear. Then she turned toward Larryboy and batted her big, beautiful eyelashes. "My, my, but you're a *dashing* cucumber," she smiled coyly. "You know, I was just saying

to my friend Jack that toilet plungers are the one fashion accessory you don't see enough of these days."

Larryboy grinned at the compliment. "Oh…well, they're not only good looking, but they're practical as…" Larryboy paused and scowled. Pointing a plunger in Outback's direction, he proclaimed, "Flattery won't help you escape the long plunger of the law."

"Perhaps not, mate, but this will!" Outback said as he aimed Jackie at Larryboy's purple noggin.

You see, Jackie is more than Outback's silly sidekick sock puppet. She is also *The Power Glove of Doom!* Inside her pretty pink hat are some of the most deadly weapons known to veggies.

Outback pushed a button on the back of his puppet, and a tiny door popped open in the side of Jackie's hat.

Larryboy had no idea what was about to hit him.

CHAPTER 3

BEE-WARE!

A tiny bee flew out of the open door in Jackie the Sock Puppet's hat—flitting and flying and landing right on Larryboy's nose.

Larryboy stared at the bee, cross-eyed.

"Why, it's just a harmless little thing," he said.

"That's what you think, mate," chuckled Outback. "Larryboy, meet the Mega Jester-Bee!"

This odd little bee aimed its stinger directly at Larryboy's face and then fired a foul cloud of green gas. As the cloud of gas completely covered Larryboy's face, the superhero went stiff as a board. When the cloud vanished, Larryboy was wearing a pair of gag glasses—complete with black horn rims and a fake nose and moustache.

Even more terrifying, Larryboy launched into an uncontrollable, rapid-fire fit of joke-telling and laughter!

"What do polar bears eat for breakfast?" Larryboy asked. "Ice Krispies!

HAHAHAHAHAHAHA! What does a 2,000-pound mouse say to a cat? Here Kitty Kitty. **HAHAHAHA-**

HAHAHA! What did the French fry say to...?"

"Oh, now why'd you have to do that?" Jackie said to Outback. "He seemed harmless enough."

"Because we don't need some vigilante veggie spoiling our plan, luv," said Outback as he yanked out a file folder marked "Top Secret." "This file is going to give us a clue to the whereabouts of the Bumblyburg Treasure."

"What goes Ha-Ha-Ha-*Thump*?" Larryboy asked, barely able to control his giggling. "A person laughing his head off! **HAHAHAHAHAHAHA!**"

File in hand, Outback Jack hopped back onto his jet-powered, boomerang-shaped glider. Flames roared from its twin engines, and Outback shot out the window.

But no one else at the *Daily Bumble* was laughing... except for Larryboy, that is.

"What do you call a boomerang that doesn't come back?" he giggled as he cornered Bob the Tomato by the water-cooler. "A stick! **HAHAHAHAHAHA!**"

"Help," Bob squeaked.

But, twenty minutes later...

"What do you get when you cross a dinosaur with a pig?" Larryboy said, following Bob the Tomato around the newspaper offices. "Jurassic pork! **HAHAHAHAHAHA!**"

"The horror," winced Bob.

And still fifteen minutes later...

"How do you clean a tuba?" Larryboy asked as he chased Bob into the lunchroom. "With a tuba toothpaste! **HAHAHAHAHAHA!**"

"**AHHHHHHHHHHHHH!**" yelled Bob.

CHAPTER 4

A SNAKE IN THE FACE

While Larryboy continued to torment Bob with an endless string of bad jokes, Outback Jack continued his own reign of terror.

First, he flipped through the stolen file until he found the information he needed about the Treasure of Bumblyburg. Then he zoomed over to the Bumblyburg Clock Tower on his glider where he tied a rope to the clock face. Jackie latched onto the rope with her mouth and yanked at the clock with all of her might.

"Pull, Jackie! Pull!" shouted Outback.

Just as the clock was finally coming loose, a voice spoke from the roof of the Clock Tower: "Your time is up, Outback!"

Outback and Jackie exchanged startled looks as they gazed at the tip-top of the tower. There, with his cape flapping gallantly in the breeze, stood Larryboy.

"What 'appened?" Outback asked.

"Run out of jokes, Laffy-boy?"

"It's *Larryboy*!" the

caped cucumber corrected. "Your laughing gas wore off a little sooner than you planned—thanks to the forty cups of water that the Bumblyburg staff threw in my face. But now the joke's on you, Outback! Knock-knock."

"Who's there?" said Outback, unable to resist a good knock-knock joke.

"Alaska."

"Alaska who?"

"Alaska one more time: Give up or you're going to taste my plungers!"

"He's good," Jackie noted.

"But not good enough, luv!"

With that, Jackie and Outback gave a mighty heave-ho, and the clock face cracked loose from the wall. Torn free, the clock dangled mid-air, connected to Outback's glider by the sturdy rope.

Quick as a cat, Larryboy fired a plunger.

THONK!

The plunger stuck fast to the clock face. Now the tug-of-war began, with Outback pulling on one end of his rope and Larryboy yanking on the other end with his plunger.

Hovering just a few feet away, Outback thrust his sock puppet forward and once again, Jackie became *The Power Glove of Doom.*

This time, however, Larryboy was ready. A flyswatter popped out of Larryboy's superhero utility belt and whipped around like a fencing foil.

"My radar-guided flyswatter will take care of your Mega Jester-Bee, Outback Jack!"

"Yer blooming right, mate," said Outback. "But it'll only make me snake veeery mad."

"Snake?" Larryboy gulped. "Did you say snake?"

Larryboy's flyswatter wilted.

"Larryboy, meet my pet rattlesnake," Outback told him as the top of Jackie's hat burst open like a spring-loaded gag-box and a real snake launched forward.

The rattlesnake flew through the air in slow motion, jaws open wide, while Larryboy sprang into action. Pressing a button on his utility belt, he triggered a weapon specially designed to fight snakes.

BOING!

Out popped a cheese grater!

"Wrong weapon, wrong weapon," Larryboy grumbled. In a panic, he pushed another button. Out popped a set of measuring cups. Then an egg beater. A frying pan. Salt and pepper shakers.

"I'm beginning to get the feeling I put on the wrong utility belt this morning," Larryboy moaned.

So, with the snake only inches from his face, Larryboy did what any superhero would do in this situation.

He ran.

Outback Jack could barely stop laughing long enough to yell, "G'day, mate!" to the fleeing cucumber. Then he and his sidekick sock puppet flew off in the opposite direction, blazing across the sky, dragging the clock face close behind.

CHAPTER 5

GUMMYBOY!

Later that day…

"I thought for sure that I set out my Larryboy Ultra-Defender Utility Belt this morning," whispered Larryboy to the superhero in the seat beside him. "But I must have set out my Mother's-Little-Helper Kitchen Utility Belt by mistake. It was very embarrassing."

"**SHHHHHHH,**" said the superhero next to him—a lemony hero known throughout the world as Lemon Twist.

Larryboy and Lemon Twist were just two of the students in a pretty extraordinary class—the Superheroes 101 Class at Bumblyburg Community College. The classroom was packed with superheroes of all shapes, sizes, and varieties. These were the amazing veggies and fruits that protected towns surrounding the entire Bumblyburg area.

"Tonight, as you know, we are going on a field trip to visit the original superheroes who once defended your towns," announced the class teacher, Bok Choy—a wise, old veggie. "We are going to visit the Bumblyburg Home for Retired Superheroes."

"Sounds like fun," whispered Larryboy to Lemon Twist. "I love field trips."

Lemon Twist tried to ignore him.

"Care for some Molar Madness?" Larryboy asked, leaning across the aisle. "It's bubblegum."

"SSSSSSHHHH," hissed Lemon Twist. "You know the rule—no gum or talking in class!"

Larryboy paused in the middle of a chew. "Oh, drat. I forgot. I better stash my gum until the end of class."

Scooping the huge wad of gum out of his mouth, Larryboy looked around for a good place to put it and finally decided that the safest place was on his utility belt. Little did he know that he'd placed the gum directly over the hole of his high-pressure air pump. A handy device if you have to pump up the tires of the Larrymobile.

"Please open your Superhero Handbook to Section 3, Paragraph 19, Line 32," Bok Choy instructed. "Perhaps Larryboy will read it for us."

"I'd be delighted," said Larryboy, picking up his Superhero Handbook. "Now, let's see, where's Section 3?" he added as he wildly flipped through his book.

Bok Choy cleared his throat. "It comes right after Section 2."

"Oh, right. I knew that," Larryboy grinned as he found the page. But in all of his moving about, he had accidentally bumped the trigger on the high-pressure air pump inside the back of his utility belt.

The bubblegum began to inflate. It grew bigger and bigger and bigger.

By the time Larryboy stood up, cleared his throat, and

began reading, "Rise in the presence of the aged. Show respect for the elderly and revere your God!" the bubblegum bubble on his belt had become the size of a basketball. But Bok Choy didn't notice because he had his back to the class as he wrote out the passage on the blackboard. Larryboy still hadn't noticed either.

But the rest of the class couldn't help but see.

There were a few snickers.

"So what does this passage mean, Larryboy?" asked Bok Choy, still scribbling on the blackboard.

"I think it means we should stand up whenever an elder superhero enters the room," Larryboy said, feeling quite pleased with himself. "Rising to your feet is a sign of respect and honor to those older and wiser."

And just as he spoke those very words, Larryboy began to rise—up in the air, his bubblegum bubble now the size of a large beach ball!

"That is correct, Larryboy," Bok Choy told him as he continued to write on the blackboard. "We can also show respect by opening doors for older people, helping them carry things, and listening to their words of wisdom. As superheroes, your elders have a wealth of knowledge and experience from which you can learn. Listen to their stories and you, too, can gain insights from their wisdom."

"How did I get up here?" Larryboy asked as he floated toward the ceiling.

"How do we revere?" Bok Choy asked, not quite clear on what Larryboy had said. "To revere your God means we are called to worship and respect him. God is all-knowing. We can trust and learn from his word, more than any other."

Bok Choy finally turned to face the class and added, "Now tell me, what else can we...?" He stopped mid-sentence and stared. Larryboy was gone. He wasn't in his seat. And he wasn't standing next to his desk.

Bok Choy's eyes drifted to the ceiling where Larryboy was floating up, up, up!

"I don't think this is what the passage meant by rising in the presence of your elders," noted Bok Choy, dryly.

At that very moment, the giant bubblegum bubble on the back of Larryboy's utility belt touched the fluorescent light on the ceiling.

POP!
CLUNK!

Larryboy dropped to the floor like a rock, completely covered with the popped bubblegum.

Larryboy sucked some of the gum back into his mouth, smacked his lips, and grinned. "Mmmmm, they're right! It's juicy and refreshing and leaves your breath minty fresh."

"Class dismissed," sighed Bok Choy.

The superheroes left the room, anxiously talking about their field trip to the Bumblyburg Home for Retired Superheroes. Unfortunately, Larryboy had to *stick* around a little longer than he had planned. After all, they didn't call it Molar Madness for nothing!

Little did Larryboy know that his sticky situations were just beginning.

CHAPTER 6

THE BALLOON BANDITS

It was time for the superheroes to take their field trip to the Bumblyburg Home for Retired Superheroes. But as the superheroes headed for the Home, time did not stand still for the dastardly doings of Outback Jack.

After stealing the clock, Outback landed his glider inside the gates of the famed Bumblyburg Balloon Factory—the greatest balloon factory in the world. The factory made everything from giant hot-air balloons to various types of balloon animals.

"It's a beauty!" said Outback Jack, staring up at a hot-air balloon that had been built on the main factory floor. The factory owners, Herbert and Wally, had taken him there to show off the balloon he'd ordered months before.

"Isn't she fantastic?" Outback asked Jackie the Sock Puppet.

Jackie was stunned. She didn't know what to say. "It *is* gorgeous! It's…it's…it's *me!*"

Jackie was right. The giant, hot-air balloon was built to look exactly like her—a giant crocodile sock puppet with a pretty pink hat.

"I'm glad you like it," said Herbert. "We have your bill all ready for you."

"And then the balloon will be yours," added Wally.

"Well...I've been meaning to talk to you blokes about that," said Outback, still staring wide-eyed at the hot-air balloon. "You see, mates, I don't have any money to give you."

Herbert and Wally exchanged glances. "No money? Then I'm afraid you can't have the balloon, Mr. Outback."

Outback finally made eye contact with the two potatoes. He had a sly smile. "I pay in different ways, mates. I have a little something socked away for times like this."

Snickering, Outback aimed his sock puppet right at Herbert and Wally. Then he pushed a button on The Power Glove of Doom.

CHAPTER 7

PRUNEMAN

Meanwhile,
Bok Choy's superhero class
piled into a school bus and drove to the
Bumblyburg Home for Retired Superheroes
on the east side of town. It was their first
field trip since the time they toured a super-
herocape factory in Puggslyville.

The retirement home was a bright, energy-
packed place. Elderly superheroes tested their old
superpowers by climbing on ceilings and walls,
while others traded stories and exchanged laughs.
There were numerous signs posted for all kinds of
amazing activities:

"HOW TO USE YOUR DENTURES TO FIGHT OFF MUTANTS."
"ROCKET-POWERED WALKERS: THE WAVE OF THE FUTURE"
"TEST YOUR X-RAY VISION AT THE WEEKLY HEALTH SCREENING."

Moving past rooms along a hallway, Bok Choy
and Larryboy spotted a large grapefruit superhero
sitting in a beach chair inside a kiddie pool. The
grapefruit calmly read the morning paper, while

gentle arches of water spouted from his head and back like a fountain.

"Hey, it's the Incredible Leaking Man!" Larryboy whispered, peeking his head into the room. "I thought he ran out of juice years ago."

"Old superheroes have more juice left in them than you think." Bok Choy divulged as he ushered Larryboy into the multi-purpose room. "Larryboy, may I present Pruneman, Bumblyburg's very first superhero."

Pruneman was…well, a prune—a little wrinkly and very old. He wore a green cape and had a large picture of a prune on his chest in bold colors. But what stood out the most were the two enormous ears attached to his mask.

Pruneman's eyes lit up at the sight of Bok Choy. "Bok Choy, you old stunt-monkey, you! How long's it been, partner?"

"Too long, my friend," said Bok Choy, as the two friends bowed to each other.

"Hey, remember that Invisible Ninja Flip you taught me?" said Pruneman, giving Bok Choy a nudge. "I can still do it after all these years!"

With those words, Pruneman went through a series of "Crouching Prune, Hidden Dragon" moves. A back flip. A tornado spin. A quick sprint up the wall. Finally, with one big burst of energy, Pruneman did a double back flip, then sprang right through the nearest door—and vanished.

Impressed, Larryboy and Bok Choy hurried through the door after him. But Pruneman was nowhere to be seen.

"WOW!" Larryboy said. "He completely disappeared!"

"Ahem," came a voice from above. "I didn't exactly dis-appear."

Larryboy and Bok Choy glanced upward. Pruneman was tangled in the chandelier.

"I've leaped, and I can't get down!" said Pruneman, wincing. "Oh, that's going to hurt in the morning. Ouch! Come to think of it, that hurts now."

CHAPTER 8
THAT'S THE PITS

Larryboy couldn't believe that Pruneman had once been Bumblyburg's number-one superhero. Why, the guy couldn't even do a simple ninja move without needing to speed-dial 911! Every student from Bok Choy's class had been paired up with a senior superhero, and Larryboy had been assigned *Pruneman*. Bok Choy said it was a great honor to have Bumblyburg's oldest superhero for a partner. But Larryboy couldn't see why. He was bored.

When Bok Choy found Larryboy, the caped cucumber was moping around by himself at the refreshment table. While, Pruneman was on the other side of the room—standing alone in front of an oscillating fan watching his cape billow in the breeze.

"Larryboy, haven't you been talking with Pruneman?" Bok Choy inquired.

"About what? The guy's a dinosaur."

"Most people think dinosaurs are pretty fascinating creatures," Bok Choy pointed out.

"You know what I mean," Larryboy said. "The only thing we have in common is that we both look good in a cape!"

At that very moment, Pruneman edged a little too close to the fan. Suddenly, the fan's blade yanked the old guy's cape with a ferocious tug and in a matter of seconds, the fan had totally shredded it up, leaving Pruneman completely capeless.

"Okay," Larryboy sighed, "now we have nothing in common," he said.

RIIINNNGGGGG! RIINNNNGGGG!

"Excuse me, Bok Choy, but my ears are ringing," Larryboy said.

It was Larryboy's Plunger-Com—a secret radio hidden inside Larryboy's plungers.

"Come in, Larryboy!" Archie's voice squeaked.

"I'm here," Larryboy told him. "What's happening, Archie?"

While Larryboy answered the call, Pruneman snatched the checkered tablecloth off the refreshment table, whipping it around his neck and turning it into his new cape. Then he moved in closer, trying to hear what Archie had to say.

"Something very strange is going on at the Bumblyburg Balloon Factory," Archie said.

"The Balloon Factory?"

"Yes. There are reports that the night shift has broken out with a serious case of bad jokes."

"That sounds like the work of Outback Jack! I'm on my way, Archie."

"Lemme help, Larryboy," pleaded Pruneman as he came up from behind him. "I can still use my famous Prune-Pit-Power-Up Move!"

"Your what?"

"My Prune-Pit-Power-Up Move! Just watch. You'll be quite impressed."

With a look of sheer determination, Pruneman began to fire prune pits—big, fat seeds—out of the large ears built into his superhero mask.

RAT-A-TAT-A-TAT-A-TAT-A-TAT!

Like a machine gun, the prune pits came out in rapid-fire fashion. But Pruneman had one little problem. His head was out of control, bouncing around like a bobble-head doll, firing prune pits in all directions.

"Hey watch it!" shouted two elderly superheroes, duck-ing underneath the folding table where they were playing checkers.

"I guess I'm a little rusty," Pruneman said, smiling awkwardly. He was feeling a bit wobbly after the prune pits finally stopped firing. "But I can still help you battle this Outback Jack character!"

Larryboy rolled his eyes as he helped Pruneman into a nearby chair. "Sorry, old fellow. But this is a job for some-one...well, someone with a little more speed and strength. Some other time, Pruneman."

As Larryboy sprinted out of the room, Pruneman watched him go with a twinge of sadness. He remembered the old days, when he had once been faster than a speeding water-melon seed...more powerful than a pumped-up papaya...able to leap tall celery in a single bound.

It didn't seem so long ago...

"Hey, Larryb—**WHHOAAAAA!**" Pruneman called out.

RAT-A-TAT-A-TAT-A-TAT-A-TAT-A-TAT!

The old guy's ears suddenly started firing prune pits again. The barrage made his chair spin like a pinwheel firework—around and around and around.

"Cut it out, Pruney!" shouted the nearby superheroes, as they ducked under their table once again.

"Ouch!"

"Incoming!"

Bok Choy looked on and sighed. Pruneman was in no shape for the perils that lay ahead.

45

CHAPTER 9

A STICKY SITUATION

The jokes were flying fast and furious at the Bumblyburg Balloon Factory.

"Why did the gum cross the road?"

"Because it was stuck to the chicken's foot."

"Why don't people play games in the jungle?"

"Too many cheetahs."

"What goes up and doesn't come down?"

"Your age."

HaHAHaHaHaHAHaHAHaHAHaHaHAHaHaHA!

The balloon factory workers rolled on the ground, holding their sides and howling with laughter. They could do nothing to stop Outback Jack, who busily connected his jeep to the bottom of the giant hot-air balloon. Mounted to the front hood of the jeep was the clock face he had ripped from the Bumblyburg Clock Tower.

Meanwhile, Larryboy was on his way to the factory in his Larryplane—a gadget-filled wonder created by his butler, Archie. In the darkness of evening, the plane hovered directly over the main factory building.

"Archie, is this the right place?" Larryboy asked over his Larryplane radio.

"Yes, I believe it is," said Archie. "My sensors are picking up a lot of laughter inside the building."

"Roger that," agreed Larryboy as he pushed a button on his instrument panel. The bottom of the Larryplane opened up to reveal rows and rows of plungers. With another push of the button, dozens of plungers rained down from the Larryplane and gripped the factory roof.

THWACK! THWACK! THWACK! THWACK!

By reeling the plungers back up toward the plane, Larryboy literally peeled off the metal roof of the factory like a pop-can tab. As he suspected, Outback was hiding inside the building, getting ready to launch his huge hot-air balloon.

"Outback, prepare to feel the sting of my plungers!" shouted Larryboy.

"Oy, mate! I'm shaking in me boots. I hate to say it, pickle boy, but you're filled with more hot air than this heeeere balloon."

Just then, a taxi came screeching up to the front door of the balloon factory. The door was thrown open—twice. (The first time, the door bounced back and closed before anyone could get out.) Eventually, Pruneman leaped out and told the taxi driver, "Keep the meter running. This won't take long." Then Pruneman hurdled forward, paused to strike a heroic pose, and ran to the factory building's front door.

Grabbing a fistful of balloons used to decorate each side of the front entrance, Pruneman quickly rose into the air. When he reached the top of the factory building, he let go of the balloons and leaped onto the roof. Even with a checkered tablecloth for a cape, Pruneman looked pretty impressive standing on top of the building, staring up at the Larryplane.

"Don't worry, Larryboy!" he shouted. "The Pit Crew has arrived!"

Larryboy groaned. This is no good. What can an old guy like Pruneman do to help?

To make matters worse, Larryboy realized he had something else to groan about—gum in the cockpit. Archie had always told him never to chew gum on a superhero mission. But he couldn't resist chewing a huge wad of Molar Madness. He also couldn't resist playing with his gum. As a result, a string of gum now connected his nose to the Larryplane controls, completely gumming up the cockpit.

Just then, Outback fired up his giant hot-air balloon and the massive ship slowly rose into the air. The expanding balloon was so huge that it barely fit through the open roof.

"Uh-oh," gulped Pruneman.

Uh-oh was right. Pruneman was standing on a narrow edge of the roof. If he wasn't careful, the balloon would bump him right off!

Outback steered the craft slightly to the right, and the giant crocodile balloon gave the ancient superhero a gentle nudge. That was all it took.

Pruneman teetered on the edge of the roof, trying to regain his balance. But all he could do was hope there'd be someone down below to catch him.

"Enjoy your fall Down Under," Outback Jack laughed.

Pruneman screamed, "*Larryboy!*" before he fell backward off the roof.

Pruneman plummeted toward the ground.

CHAPTER 10

IT GETS EVEN STICKIER

Pruneman was forty feet from the ground and falling fast.

Larryboy had to act quickly. But that was easier said than done. His string of gum had now turned into five strings of sticky stuff, creating a bubblegum web inside the cockpit.

The caped cucumber pressed the Larryplane joystick, and the plane dove down toward the falling prune. But Larryboy was so busy untangling himself from the gum that he nearly drove the Larryplane right into the side of the balloon factory.

Pruneman was thirty feet from the ground.

There were now ten strings of sticky gum connecting the controls to Larryboy's face.

"Plungers away!"

Larryboy managed to fire two plungers at Pruneman, but having to shoot through the maze of gum, one of them hit the side of the building and stuck. Still connected to the plunger's tether line, it caused the plane to whip around the building like a carnival ride.

Pruneman was twenty-one feet, four and one half inches from the ground.

Larryboy had only one hope left—a heat-seeking plunger that Archie had just invented. It had never been used before.

Pruneman was thirteen feet from the ground.

"That's roughly four meters in metric measurements!" Pruneman yelled as he fell.

POW! ZIP!

The heat-seeking plunger tore through the tangle of gum and streaked across the sky.

Pruneman was only three feet from the ground.

THWACK!

The heat-seeking plunger hit Pruneman smack in the middle of his back and stopped his fall just in time.

"Nice gadget," Pruneman noted, as he dangled just two inches from the cement. "We've got a toilet backing up in the lounge you might want to look at."

Although he was pleased he had saved the old superhero, Larryboy was frustrated beyond belief. Outback Jack and his Balloon of Doom had vanished into the dark night, and Larryboy was in no shape to pursue him. Twenty-five strings of gum now crisscrossed the cockpit, and even more gum decorated the upholstery.

Larryboy had just enough gum left to blow a bubble, but it popped in his face.

"Drat."

CHAPTER 11

CLUES AND CONNECTIONS

The next morning at the
Daily Bumble newspaper, Bob the
Tomato called an urgent meeting. Vicki,
the staff's top photographer, was there,
along with cub reporter, Junior Asparagus.
Larry the Janitor was mopping the floor...
...and listening.

Little did they know that mild-mannered Larry
the Janitor was really Larryboy! You see, Larryboy
was the only superhero with two secret identities.
Sometimes he was Lawrence, the fantastically rich,
courteous cucumber; and other times, he was Larry the
Janitor.

"Outback Jack stole my research file on the town's
founding fathers," Bob explained to his staff as he
paced the floor.

"And then he stole the town clock," said Vicki.

"And he stole a giant hot-air balloon," added
Junior.

"What's the connection?" asked Bob.

"I know!" shouted Larry the Janitor, wheeling around to face Bob and accidentally knocking Junior out of his seat with his mop handle. "They all have to do with *saving*!"

"Saving?" asked Vicki.

"Yes!" Larry shouted, wheeling around to face his favorite photographer. But as he gazed into Vicki's attractive eyes, he accidentally smacked Bob out of his seat with the mop handle. "You 'save' things in a research file."

"Yeah, but what about the clock?" Junior reminded him.

"A clock tells time! And you can 'save' time," Larry exclaimed. He wheeled around to face Junior and nearly swept Vicki off her chair with his mop handle. She ducked just in time.

"Then what about the hot-air balloon?" asked Vicki. "What does it have to do with 'saving'?"

Larry paused and stared blankly at Vicki. "Well…er…a hot-air balloon contains…um…air…and air is something that planes fly through…and…um…when a plane turns right, it is called 'banking' to the right. And a bank is where you keep money that you…um…'save.'" Larry smiled weakly.

"You don't really know how the balloon connects to the other things, do you?" asked Bob.

"Not a clue."

Suddenly, Larryboy's mop began to beep. Bob, Vicki, and Junior blinked in surprise.

"Your mop is beeping," Junior pointed out.

"Uh…yes," said Larry, staring awkwardly at his chirping mop. "My…uh…my automatic spill detector has automatically detected a spill. Gotta go!"

Larry the Janitor dashed out of the room, scurried into the janitor closet, and plopped the string mop over his head. Dirty water dripped down his face. He made a note to squeeze the water out of the mop *before* covering his head with his radio mop the next time.

"Hello, Master Lawrence." Archie's voice came through a screen that illuminated under the mop. The flickering image was of the asparagus butler standing in front of a panel of computerized equipment. "Bok Choy called to remind you to finish your superhero class assignment."

"Aw, but Archie," whined Larry. "I hate spending time with Pruneman. He's so out of touch. Pruneman messed up everything yesterday. If he hadn't tried to help, Outback never would have gotten away."

"May I remind you about the gum?"

"Point taken. But Pruneman is *so old*. Can't you tell Bok Choy I'm too busy to go to the retirement home?"

"After the bubblegum incident in class yesterday, he said your grade depends on this," said Archie.

"I'll be there in ten minutes."

Twenty minutes later, Larryboy was back in the halls of the Bumblyburg Home for Retired Superheroes. He paused in front of a sign that said, "Today: Superhero Bingo."

"Hey, maybe this won't be so bad after all," Larryboy said to himself. "After all, I like Bingo."

Larryboy pushed open the door to the multi-purpose room, expecting a calm game of Bingo with the old folks. Just a nice, easy-going, quiet...

POW! KA-BLOOEY! SWOOSH! BA-BOOM! RAT-A-TAT!

Entering the room, Larryboy was greeted by an explosion of noise. Superhero weapons were firing from every corner.

CHAPTER 12

LASERS AND LIGHTNING AND LINT, OH MY!

Lasers streaked across the multi-purpose room. So did lightning bolts, streams of extra-hot taco sauce, snowballs, grappling hooks, bungee cords, sock lint, harpoons, and ping-pong balls.

Diving for cover, Larryboy made his way underneath the walkers, chairs, and tables, while deadly objects flew through the air right above him. It was like being in a war zone. Larryboy eventually squirmed his way to where Pruneman was sitting.

"Larryboy!" Pruneman shouted happily, looking down at his purple friend. "What a surprise! Wanna play Superhero Bingo with me!"

"This is Bingo?" Larryboy asked, crawling up and onto a chair. The weapons had finally stopped firing. "I thought Bingo was...uh...a quieter game."

"Not with superheroes," chuckled Pruneman. "See those giant Bingo cards over there by the wall?"

Larryboy nodded. On the far wall was a line of enormous Bingo cards. The cards were splattered, charred, and stuck with just about every superhero weapon imaginable—from mud-bombs and ice cream to darts and fireballs.

"My card is the third one from the left," said Pruneman. "If they call a number that's on my card, I fire my prune pits at it. I have to hit just the right spot on the card for it to count," Pruneman giggled. "Unfortunately, a lot of us don't have the aim we used to have."

So true. Most of the shots were way off the mark. A lot of the superhero weapons misfired and missed the target altogether, doing deep damage to the wall behind the cards. In fact, an entire section of the multi-purpose room's wall was missing.

"B-4," said a voice over the intercom.

"That's me!" shouted Pruneman, jumping out of his chair.

Weapons fired from all sides.

POW! KA-BLOOEY! SWOOSH! BA-BOOM! RAT-A-TAT! CLICK, CLICK, CLICK.

Pruneman tried to fire prune seeds from his ear, but nothing came out.

"Aw fiddlepits!" he said. "I've got B-4, but I'm fresh out of pit power." Pruneman turned to Larryboy. "Quick, fire a plunger for me at B-4."

"Huh?"

"Fire a plunger at B-4 on my Bingo card! If I win this game, I'll get an all-expense paid trip to Flimflamhamshire for the annual polyester harvest!"

Larryboy stood up and stared at the Bingo card—like a gunslinger sizing up his enemy. His eyes narrowed as he took aim.

FWAPPPP!

Larryboy's plunger zipped across the room, threading its way through the barrage of weapons.

THWACK!

The plunger hit dead center on B-4.

"Hot diggity!" Pruneman shouted, jumping into the air. "Larryboy, you're a natural at this game!"

"Nice shot, young fellow!" said an elderly superhero carrot from his rocking chair—which hovered in mid-air.

"That's my partner," said Pruneman proudly. He smiled at Larryboy.

As a couple of other senior superheroes nodded their approval, a smile grew on Larryboy's face. He was actually beginning to like this.

Even more surprising, he was beginning to like Pruneman.

CHAPTER 13

A BLAST FROM THE PAST

Later that day, Larryboy rose from his chair as Pruneman strolled into the room, carrying a photo album.

What an afternoon it had been. After three rip-roaring games of Superhero Bingo, Larryboy and Pruneman spent the rest of the afternoon scaling walls and trying out a new supercharged wheelchair. It was the only wheelchair in the world with a jet engine, helicopter blades, a smoke screen, and a laser-guided Slushie-tossing slingshot.

Larryboy didn't know that an old guy could be so much fun.

When the afternoon of action was over, Pruneman invited Larryboy to the retirement home's Clock Room for a glass of iced tea—and a peek at an old photo album.

"This Clock Room is an amazing place," Larryboy said, glancing around at the hundreds of clocks lining every wall. There were grandfather clocks, water clocks, cuckoo clocks, and an entire shelf-load of hourglasses filled with sand.

"The fellow who built our retirement home was really fascinated by time," Pruneman noted. "Maybe that's why he was so interested in us old folks. We've all seen a lot of time go by."

Pruneman opened up the photo album and spread it out on a coffee table. "Speaking of time, here's the photo I wanted to show you. It's from a long time ago."

The black and white photo showed a much younger Pruneman blasting a volley of prune pits at a supervillain perched high atop the Clock Tower.

"WOW!" exclaimed Larryboy. "Is that you fighting the Evil Squashinator?"

"Sure is."

"I heard all about the Squashinator—a giant robotic squash that had been programmed to squash all the buildings in Bumblyburg by sitting on them. Was it you who defeated the Squashinator?"

Pruneman blushed. "Yes, it was. But that's not why I wanted to show you this photo."

Larryboy's eyes lit up. Who would have thought that an old guy like Pruneman had once been a young hero capable of defeating the Squashinator? Why, if it hadn't been for Pruneman, Bumblyburg wouldn't even exist today!

"I wanted to show you this photo because it might shed some light on what Outback Jack is up to."

"Really?"

"Maybe. You said that Outback Jack stole a file and then he stole the town clock, right?"

Larryboy nodded, eager for Pruneman to go on.

"Well, there's an old legend that the town clock originally belonged to Sir Lester Bumbly and Sir Mortimer Burg."

"Bumblyburg's founding fathers!" Larryboy gasped. "Bob was going to do an article about them before Outback stole his research file."

"Legend has it that they hid their family fortune to keep it away from attacking pirates. There's even a story that says they painted a secret map to the treasure on the face of the town clock."

Pruneman held a magnifying glass over the photo of the Clock Tower, while Larryboy took a close look. On the clock face were lots of fancy pictures surrounding the numbers. At the very top, above the number twelve, was a drawing of three hills—with a rock structure built upon the one in the middle. A stream of sunlight passed straight through a hole in the center of it.

"Those are the three hills on the edge of Bumblyburg," Larryboy said, whistling. "And I recognize that rock structure—it's the Rock of Time. Do you think this is the treasure map?"

Pruneman nodded solemnly.

"But how do you know all this?"

"You live. You listen. You learn," Pruneman explained, solemnly.

Larryboy stood up straight and looked very heroic. "Well, if Outback Jack is using that clock map to steal the Treasure of Bumblyburg, then it's my job to foil his evil plan!"

As Larryboy made a move to leap through the nearest window, Pruneman tried to stop him. "But wait, Larryboy! There's one other important thing you need to know!"

"No time for that, Pruneman! I AM THAT HERO!"

"But Larryboy...You need to know..."

Too late. Larryboy was already out the window and leaping into his Larrymobile. Time does not wait for a superhero on the move.

CHAPTER 14

WHALLOPING WALLABEES!

Evening crept across the city of Bumblyburg. But despite the darkening hours, Bumbly Park in the center of town was still packed with veggies. Some were walking their dogs. Others were taking their daily jog. And a number of elderly veggies were playing chess.

Above them, an ominous shadow drifted across the park like an evil cloud. It was the shadow of a hot-air balloon floating across the sky. Most veggies thought it was a strange sight on this clear, beautiful evening. And there was one very odd thing about the balloon— instead of a basket, a jeep was connected to its bottom.

Little did they know...

Outback rode through the air in his floating jeep, staring off into the distance toward three hills. On top of the middle hill was the famous rock structure, the Rock of Time.

"There they are, luv," he told his sock puppet. "The three hills.

And unless I'm mistaken, we'll find out where the treasure is buried right about *now*."

As the sun dipped behind the hills, it moved into just the right spot for a beam of sunlight to shoot through the hole in the center of the Rock of Time. Like a golden laser, the sunlight beam shot straight down from the hillside and struck the statue of Sir Lester Bumbly, located in the very center of the park.

"Blimey," said Outback, his eyes glittering. "The beam points right to the spot where the treasure is hidden. It must be buried beneath the statue."

"We're going to be rich!" Jackie shrieked.

"Time to start diggin'," said Outback. "But first, we need to clear the park, luv."

Raising a megaphone to his mouth, Outback leaned over the edge of his jeep. "Citizens of Bumblyburg," he called to the veggies far below. "Go home. Get out of the park...*now*!"

The veggies looked at each other in confusion. Several dogs barked at the hot-air balloon. Ma Mushroom stared up and yelled, "Whippersnapper!"

"Why should we leave the park just because you say

so?" said a middle-aged carrot.

"Who do you think you are?" shouted a pea.

"We're in the middle of a chess game!" yelled an elderly asparagus.

Outback Jack sighed and looked his sock puppet in the eyes. "Well, Jackie, we can't say we didn't warn them."

"If you don't leave *now*, I'll be forced to release me outback wall-a-bees," Outback Jack warned them.

But no one appeared frightened.

"Wallabies? Aren't they cute little kangaroos?" asked Herbert who was having lunch in the park with Wally.

"I think so. I'm not afraid of a wallaby," answered Wally.

"I warned ya!" shouted Outback Jack. "Here's me wall-a-bees!"

Jackie's pillbox hat opened at once, and a swarm of bees flew out and swooped down on the veggies in Bumbly Park.

"Oh! A wall of *bees*," cried Herbert and Wally as they scurried back to the factory.

But not everyone was afraid. In fact, several veggies got out cans of high-powered bee repellent and continued on with their jogging and chess games.

"Do we get to croc 'em, now?" Jackie asked, dancing with delight.

"Yes, luv! Time to croc 'em!"

Outback pushed a button on a remote-control device, and a huge door opened on the side of the huge hat on top of the huge hot-air balloon. (Remember, the balloon looked just like Jackie.) Out dropped...

One crocodile.

Two crocodiles.

Three crocodiles.

Four. Five. Six. Seven.

With parachutes attached to their scaly backs, the crocodiles fell to earth like reptilian bombs. But these weren't ordinary crocs. They were *hungry* crocodiles. Mean crocs. For three straight days, they had been forced to listen to a CD of the Bumblyburg Yodeling Club, so they were looking for someone to bite.

Vegetable stew sounded good to them.

"AHHHHHHHHHHHHHHHH!"

As the crocs hit the ground running, Veggies scattered in all directions, running out of the park as fast they could.

"Check, mate!" Outback shouted to the elderly guys who finally fled their chess game.

"AHHHHHHHHHHHHHHHH!"

Outback's plan was running like clockwork.

CHAPTER 15

THE CROCS TAKE OVER

Larryboy was startled by
the wall of fleeing veggies as he
raced his Larrymobile toward the center
of town.

"What's going on?" he called to three running scallions.

"Crocodiles have taken over Bumbly Park!" shouted one scallion. "Run for your life!"

Putting his foot to the floor, the Larrymobile shot forward. When Larryboy reached the park, he could see that an army of crocodiles had made a circle around the statue of Sir Lester Bumbly.

All the veggies had fled—except Ma Mushroom. She wasn't going to budge. She was determined to sit and eat her three-scoop ice cream cone in peace. When a crocodile came at her, Ma Mushroom gave it a blistering look. Knowing better, the croc retreated, whimpering like a scolded puppy.

Meanwhile, Outback Jack drifted down from
the sky in his hot-air balloon. As you recall
(you'll be tested on this), Outback's jeep dangled from the bottom of the balloon. But what

you probably didn't know was that a mechanical digging device was attached to the front end.

"Be careful, Larryboy," Archie called out over the Larrymobile radio. "That giant Jackie balloon could be outfitted with dastardly secret weapons."

"I'm ready for any secret weapon he's got, Archie."

THWACK! THWACK! THWACK!

The Larrymobile fired three X-42 mega-plungers at the nearest crocodiles, allowing the superhero to slip past them.

"Good shot, Larryboy!" boomed a voice from some-where above.

Glancing up over his shoulder, Larryboy was shocked to see Pruneman—flying! Evidently, Pruneman had finally mastered his Prune-Pit-Power-Up Move. Prune pits streamed out of the large down-turned ears on his cos-tume mask, propelling him forward at incredible speed.

Larryboy had a sinking feeling. The last time Pruneman tried to help, he had messed up everything. Pruneman was just too old for this kind of thing.

Larryboy opened his cockpit and shouted, "You're flying? Isn't that a little dangerous at your age?"

"No problemo," grinned Pruneman. "Flying is like riding a bike. Once you learn, you never forget. Once you...**WHOOOOAAAAAAAAA!**" Suddenly, Pruneman's stream of prune pits went berserk. The elderly superhero started to zig when he was supposed to zag.

"Come to think of it, I never did learn how to ride a bike!" Pruneman shouted as he roared out of control, skimming just two feet over Ma Mushroom's head.

"Whippersnapper!"

Larryboy quickly positioned the Larrymobile beneath Outback's hot-air balloon and fired a plunger, which arced upward about fifty feet. The plunger connected with the door of Outback's jeep.

THWACK!

Larryboy scrambled up the tether line, climbing all of the way up to the door of the jeep. There he found himself staring into the face of pure evil—Jackie the Sock Puppet!

"Cease your villainous..." Larryboy started to say.

"Oh, shove off!" scoffed Outback.

Outback Jack simply flung his door open and Larryboy, who was hanging on to the door, was flung back as well. He was smashed like a bug against the side of the jeep.

"OOOOFFF!"

"Are you all right, Larryboy?" called Archie over the plunger-com. "What happened?"

"I forgot the old 'car door' trick," Larryboy answered in a pinched voice.

Larryboy's plunger suddenly popped loose from the door. Then his eyes crossed as he slid down the side of the jeep and tumbled to earth.

Larryboy yelled: **"PRUNEMAN!"**

That was his last word before the purple, plunger-pelting hero plummeted. (Try saying that ten times really fast.)

CHAPTER 16

UN-BEE-LIEVABLE!

Larryboy was fifty feet from the ground and falling fast.

"Don't fear, Larryboy! Help is on the way!" Pruneman shouted.

Only one problem. Pruneman was still having a hard time getting his Prune-Pit-Power-Up Move under control. He dipped. He barrel-rolled. He loop-de-looped. He nearly crashed a dozen times.

Larryboy was now forty-five feet from the ground.

At last, Pruneman got his target in sight. Weaving like a bird that had lost its flying permit, Pruneman swooped down and scooped up...

Ma Mushroom?

"Oops," said Pruneman.

"What's the big idea, whippersnapper!" shouted Ma Mushroom. She had been minding her own business, eating her three-scoop ice cream cone. Now she found herself scooped up, perched on Pruneman's back, taking the ride of her life.

"Sorry, Ma,"

said Pruneman. "I thought you were Larryboy."

"How could you mistake me for a hairy boy?" scowled Ma Mushroom. "You're just lucky my ice cream cone is still in one piece."

Ma Mushroom peered at Pruneman over the top of her glasses. "You've got prune pits coming out of your ears," she noted in disbelief. Then, as an afterthought, she said, "Pretty cool."

Meanwhile, Larryboy was now twenty feet from the ground. In a few more moments, he was going to be Pancake-Boy.

"WHOOOOOAAAA NELLIE!" yelled Ma Mushroom as Pruneman made a sharp turn, reversing direction. One of her ice cream scoops popped up in the air, but she caught it before it fell.

The out-of-control Pruneman roared through two back-yards, plucking a laundry line of clothes clear out of the ground. Then he bore right through a large quilt, creating a mushroom-shaped hole.

"I've got lint on my ice cream," Ma Mushroom complained. "Watch it, sonny!"

Just seconds before Larryboy hit the ground, Pruneman finally regained control of his prune-pit stream. But he still wasn't close enough to pluck Larryboy out of the air.

THWOPP! THWACK!

Just in time, Larryboy fired off a plunger, which attached itself to Ma Mushroom's face. The line held and Larryboy was pulled up, up into the air, and towed behind the flying Pruneman.

"Whippersnapper!" Ma Mushroom's muffled voice came from inside the plunger.

Larryboy was saved! That was the good news.

The bad news was that while all of this was happening, the hot-air balloon had landed and Outback Jack had gone digging. He had already ripped out the statue and was chewing into the soil.

"We gotta stop them!" Larryboy shouted, while being dragged across the sky.

"Don't worry, Larryboy, I'm on it," said Pruneman.

Carrying Ma Mushroom, dragging Larryboy, and trailing a laundry-line of clothes, Pruneman changed directions and raced straight for Outback.

"The old geezer and that purple guy are heading our way," said Jackie the Sock Puppet as Outback hurried to retrieve the treasure.

"Blimey, they don't give up, do they? Well—you know what must be done."

"Sure do," said Jackie.

Jackie poked a button on Outback's remote control. Then the lid opened on the huge pink hat that sat on top of the huge crocodile balloon. Out came the largest insect imaginable. It looked like a prehistoric bug.

It was a *giant* Mega Jester-Bee, and it was headed straight for our heroes!

CHAPTER 17

THE SANDS OF TIME

"Our awesome Aussie bee will keep those blokes busy for awhile," explained Outback, tearing into the ground with his digging device.

CLUNK!

"I think you've hit something, Jack!" said the sock puppet. "And it sounds like metal."

"That's the sound of a bloomin' treasure chest, luv! That's also the sound of us getting rich!"

Sure enough, the mechanical shovel dug deeply, lifting out two humongous chests. Then it dropped them to the ground, along with a load of dirt and sod.

"Me treasure!" Jackie sang out. "I'm going to buy a pony! I'm going to buy a pony!"

Leaping from his jeep, Outback grabbed a crowbar, stuck it into the treasure chest latch, and yanked. The chest cracked open like an oyster. Breathless, Outback threw back the lid. He couldn't believe he was about to become rich beyond his wildest dreams. He stepped back and feasted his eyes on the glorious wonders of...

Sand?

Outback lifted out a scoop of what was supposed to be gold. But it wasn't. The treasure chest was filled with beach sand. In a panic, Outback cracked open the second chest—and found more of the same. Sand, sand, sand!

He overturned the chests, hoping to find jewels buried beneath the sand. But there was nothing!

"We've been duped, luv!"

"I could have told you there'd be no treasure under that statue," said someone nearby.

Outback wheeled around and found himself staring at Pruneman, Larryboy, and Ma Mushroom. Our heroes were back on level ground, ready to make an arrest.

"I knew there was no treasure buried here in the park," repeated Pruneman.

"You did?" Larryboy asked, just as surprised as Outback.

"Yes. I tried to tell you back at the retirement home," Pruneman explained. "But you took off before I had a chance."

"My bad," said Larryboy.

"Isn't it time for your nap, Prunejuiceman?" Outback snarled at the old hero.

Larryboy's blood boiled. "You've got a lot of nerve calling him Prunejuiceman. Pruneman is a hero! He's been saving people since before you were born."

"He's an old coot."

"Rise in the presence of the aged, show respect for the elderly, and revere your God," Larryboy said, repeating the words from Bok Choy's class.

"What in the world are you blabbing about?" Outback scoffed.

"We should show respect to our elders," said Larryboy. "Respect! That's spelled 'R-E-S-P-E-C-T.'"

Suddenly, Jackie the Sock Puppet burst out in song. "R-E-S-P-E-C-T! Tell me what it means to me! R-E-S-P-E-C-T! Sock it to me, sock it to me, sock it to me, sock it…"

"Stuff a sock in it, Jackie!" Outback yelled.

"Sorry. I always get carried away by that song."

Outback turned his back on Larryboy, furious. "The only thing I'm going to show you and Pruneman is a good thrashing, mate. And when I'm done, I'm going to tear this city apart until I find that bloomin' treasure."

"And how do you plan to do that?" asked Pruneman.

(This is the part where the evil villain unwittingly gives away his plan.)

"After my Mega Jester-Bee sprays laughing gas on the entire city, no one will be able to stop me," laughed Outback. "I'll go house to house and building to building until I find that treasure! Blimey, you blokes just don't get it, do you?"

Larryboy turned and gazed toward downtown Bumblyburg. Sure enough, Outback's evil plan was already hatching.

The big bad bee dive-bombed the city, spraying its cloud of green gas like a crop duster. As the green gas settled on the city, hundreds of veggie citizens suddenly found themselves wearing gag glasses with silly attached noses and moustaches. Bad jokes would abound as Outback Jack buzzed through the city in search of the treasure.

It was no laughing matter.

CHAPTER 18

POP! GOES THE WEASELS

Before Ma Mushroom
could even mutter, "whippersnapper,"
Pruneman, the elderly superhero raced to
the rescue. With his checkered tablecloth
cape flapping in the wind, he swooped down
on the giant bee, zipping within inches of the
creature's giant eyes.

The bee's attention was taken away from the
city—just for a moment.

Pruneman zipped by the big bee a second time.

By the third time, the monster was furious. The
senior superhero was pestering the giant bee in the
same way that bees pester veggies during sweet sum-
mer picnics.

Turning away from the city's downtown, the giant
bee took off after Pruneman.

"Say goodbye to the old coot, Larryboy," Outback
said as they watched the scene unfold from a distance. "That bloomin' bee is going to finish him
off! As for me, I'm heading into town to find me
some treasure. G'day, mate."

Outback hopped into his hot-air balloon

and prepared for takeoff. But if Outback had been a little wiser, he might have realized what Pruneman was trying to do. He wasn't just luring the bee away from Bumblyburg. He was luring the bee *toward* Outback.

Pruneman raced across the sky, with the bloated bee just several feet behind him. If it hadn't been for a couple of quick dodges, the monster might have had him. Instead, Pruneman zeroed in on the hot-air balloon, which was just beginning to rise from the ground.

SWOOOOOSHHHHH!
BUZZZZZZZZZZZZZ!

Pruneman and the bee cut a path right past Outback's balloon.

"Blimey, what was that?" Outback said, looking up.

"I don't like the looks of this," cried Jackie.

SWOOOOOSHHHHH!
BUZZZZZZZZZZZZZ!

"Oy, that was close!" Outback grumbled, getting a little nervous.

On the third pass, Pruneman shouted to Larryboy. "Use your plungers, Larryboy!"

Larryboy took aim. He fired.

THONK!

The plunger struck home, hitting the bee square in the forehead. With startling power, the force of the plunger sent the giant bee reeling backward, tumbling toward the hot-air balloon, stinger first.

POP!

The giant stinger sank deep into the balloon. Air

escaped so fast that the balloon whipped around with the big bee's stinger still lodged inside.

"Hang on, Jackie!" yelled Outback.

"AHHHHHHHHH!" screamed the sock puppet.

The punctured balloon shot off into the distance, zipping up and down, back and forth, and to and fro (wherever "fro" is). The balloon made the kind of wild moves that you might expect on one of the Ten-Rides-Most-Likely-to-Make-You-Wish-You-Hadn't-Eaten-a-Big-Breakfast.

When all the air had finally leaked out, the balloon crash-landed just feet from Officer Olaf and his paddy wagon.

Special delivery.

"I'm sorry I let you down, luv," said Outback Jack to his sock puppet as the officer tossed the villains into the paddy wagon. "I tried my best, but Prunejuiceman was sharper than I thought."

Jackie simply turned away in a huff. "Talk to the hand, Outback. Talk to the hand."

"Watch it, luv. You were just dirty laundry before I came along. I *made* you!"

Officer Olaf slammed the paddy wagon door closed with a deafening **CLANG!**

CHAPTER 19

THE GOLDEN YEARS

With Outback and Jackie behind bars, the city of Bumblyburg was safe and sound once again. Veggies poured out of their homes and offices, cheering Larryboy for what he had done. But Larryboy gave the credit to Pruneman.

"Pruneman?" asked many of the veggies. "Never heard of him. He must be some new superhero."

"He doesn't look new. Looks pretty ancient."

If only they knew...

Far into the night, the celebrations continued. In fact, Larryboy and Pruneman didn't even get a chance for some well-deserved rest until long after their bedtimes.

By the next day, Larryboy was feeling as good as new and was eager to visit Pruneman at the Home for Retired Superheroes. Only this time, he didn't have to be forced to go.

"We made a good team, didn't we?" said Larryboy, casting his eyes at the clocks in the Clock Room.

"We sure did," agreed Pruneman.

"But you know, it doesn't seem fair," said Larryboy.

"What doesn't seem fair?"

"Over your long life, you've rescued this city again and again, Pruneman. But people always forget. Even *I* forgot what you did for us so long ago. It shouldn't take something like this for people to remember—and respect you."

"Time passes," Pruneman said. "I try not to let it bother me."

"Show respect for the elderly and revere your God," Larryboy said to himself, trying not to forget the words from his *Superhero Handbook*. "By the way, if the Treasure of Bumblyburg wasn't under the statue of Sir Lester Bumbly, then where is it hidden?"

Pruneman grinned. "I'm sorry, Larryboy, but I promised I would keep it a secret. I'm afraid I cannot tell *even* you."

Larryboy shrugged good-naturedly. "That's OK. I wouldn't want you to break your promise. Say, how about a game of Superhero Bingo?"

"I'd love it."

As Larryboy bounced out of the Clock Room, Pruneman paused to glance around. His eyes fell on the hourglasses lining one of the walls, and he smiled.

Sand flowed from one end of the hourglasses to the other. But if someone had taken the time to look carefully, he or she would have noticed that the sand in the hourglasses flashed with glints of gold.

Time is golden. Time is truly a treasure from God. Just ask any senior superhero.

Pruneman closed the door to the Clock Room and hurried after Larryboy.

"WE ARE THOSE HEROES!" shouted the dynamic duo as they bounded into the multi-purpose room, side by side.

THE END

VeggieTales

LARRYBOY™

AND THE YODELNAPPER

WRITTEN BY
KENT REDEKER

ILLUSTRATED BY
MICHAEL MOORE

BASED ON THE HIT VIDEO SERIES: LARRYBOY
CREATED BY PHIL VISCHER
SERIES ADAPTED BY TOM BANCROFT

ZONDERkidz

ZONDERVAN.com/
AUTHORTRACKER
follow your favorite authors

TABLE OF CONTENTS

CHAPTER 1

HULA HEIDI HAZARD

Mayor Fleming was not at work. She had taken the day off. She was skipping merrily through a field of tulips while gleefully warbling a made-up tune about marmalade and beach balls.

Why would the mayor of Bumblyburg act in such a footloose and fancy-free way? Because it was a splendidly gorgeous day in Bumblyburg! It was the kind of day where you could almost smell the happiness and carefree-icity in the air—the kind of day where you wonder why anyone would ever stay indoors doing algebra problems.

Good citizens all over Bumblyburg were enjoying the fine morning. Herbert and Wally were grilling cheese-filled hot dogs. Junior Asparagus was waterskiing. Even Police Chief Croswell had decided to enjoy the day by hang gliding off Mount Bumbly while eating a very large snow cone.

But what was Larry the Cucumber doing on this fine, happy, happy spring day? Larry and his faithful butler, Archie, were doing something decidedly unhappy and unspringlike. They were waiting in line.

More specifically, they were standing in line outside of Mr. Snappy's Extremely Gigantic Toy Emporium (which is an unnecessarily long way of saying Mr. Snappy's Great-Big Toy Store).

Why would Larry, or anyone else for that matter, be standing in line on such a fine day? The answer is simple: Hula Heidi.

"I can't wait to get my very own Hula Heidi doll!" said Larry. Hula Heidi was the latest in the Hula Friends line of dolls. Each doll played Hawaiian music and danced its own version of the hula. Since it was the first day anyone could buy Hula Heidi, dozens of Hula Friends lovers were waiting outside the toy store so that they could be among the first to buy one.

"But Master Larry," said Archie. "It's such a beautiful warbling sort of morning! Wouldn't you rather be out skipping through the fields?"

"Archie! I'm surprised at you!" said Larry. "You know how much I want a new Hula Friend. They do the hula…like this!" He began humming Hawaiian music and dancing his own little hula. **"ALOAH-AH-OOOY! AL-WAA-LEE-LOO!"** Unfortunately, Larry's attempt at dancing looked more like a worm trying to put on a leotard than an actual hula dance.

"Yes, yes," said Archie. "I know. But don't you think you might already have *enough* Hula Friends?"

Larry looked shocked. "You don't understand, Archie," answered Larry. "I may have Hula Hillary and Hula Howie and Hula Hannah and Hula Hattie and Hula Harley and Hula Heather and Hula Harry and Hula Henrietta and Hula Hector and Hula Holly and Hula Harriet and Hula Hortence and Hula Hank and Hula Hallie and…and some others, I think, but I don't have Hula *Heidi*. And if I don't have Hula Heidi, I won't have them all, and I *have* to have them *all*!"

CHAPTER 2

STAMPEDE!

At that moment, Archie was just about to tell Larry that he did *not* need them all. In fact Archie was about to say that Larry was spending way too much time playing with his Hula Friends. Archie knew that God doesn't want us to center our lives on material things. He thought Larry should spend more time with his family and his friends. He was even about to say that perhaps it wasn't healthy for someone like Larry to play for days in the basement talking to dolls while wearing a grass skirt and drinking coconut milk.

These are things that Archie wanted to say. But all he ever got the chance to say was **"OOOF,"** for at that moment, the doors of Mr. Snappy's Extremely Gigantic Toy Emporium opened. All of the Hula Friends lovers who had been standing in line pushed and shoved and stomped and stampeded right past Archie, knocking him flat on his stalk!

It was total madness as the most frenzied toy buyers in all of Bumblyburg rushed into the store. Each one of them wanted to be the first to buy a Hula Heidi. They pushed and they shoved. It was the worst pushing and shoving ever seen in Bumblyburg!

Larry found himself near the back of the line. To get closer to the front, he grabbed a pogo stick and attempted to bounce forward. He called, **"I'M COMING, HULA HEIDI!"**

Larry was so excited that he didn't even notice that one of his pogo-bounces knocked a Young Scientist Chemistry Set to the floor. All of the bottles of chemicals broke open, and the contents became mixed together. The mess trickled across the floor, where it oozed into an exhibit—*The World's Biggest Lump of Crazy Clay*. When the chemicals reached the huge lump of Crazy Clay, a strange and unexpected thing began to happen. It was the kind of thing that you never would have guessed: the chemicals caused a reaction that turned The World's Biggest Lump of Crazy Clay into The World's Biggest Lump of Crazy Clay That Could Move Around Like A Giant Amoeba And Liked To Smash Things!

CHAPTER 3

CRAZY CLAY GONE CRAZY

The World's Biggest Lump of Crazy Clay rose up and smashed a whole shelf full of tricycles. The noise was so loud that even the stampeding Hula Heidi lovers stopped to look.

"AAAAAAUGH!" said one of the stampeders. "The World's Biggest Lump of Crazy Clay has gone...**CRAZY!"**

Instead of customers rushing to buy toys, customers were now rushing to get away from the giant blue lump of Crazy Clay. It was bad. It was the worst catastrophe that had ever happened at a toy store in Bumblyburg.

"We need a hero of some sort!" shouted Mr. Snappy, the toy-store owner.

Larry realized that this was a job for Bumblyburg's favorite cucumber crime crusader!

He dove under a pile of stuffed animals—but not to hide like a frightened little baby chick. No siree! Moments later he burst forth from the pile as...*Larryboy!*

"I...AM...THAT...HERO!" shouted Larryboy.

Meanwhile, The World's Biggest Lump of Crazy Clay continued to smash its way through the store. Since they were in a toy store, toys were the things that were getting smashed the most. The Crazy Clay picked up a dollhouse and prepared to throw it to the ground.

Larryboy hopped in front of the Crazy Clay. He wasn't about to sit by and let an innocent dollhouse get smashed needlessly.

"Halt, World's Biggest Lump of Crazy Clay!" he shouted. "I don't know why you are so angry with these toys, but I'm sure we can talk about whatever it is that's making you so mad."

The dollhouse came crashing down on Larryboy's head. Apparently the Crazy Clay was in no mood to talk.

"That does it!" said a slightly woozy Larryboy. "Taste my plungers, blob creature!"

Larryboy fired his miraculous plunger ears at The World's Biggest Lump of Crazy Clay. But instead of defeating the creature, the plungers went right through it. The Crazy Clay made a horrible gurgling noise.

That's when Larryboy realized two things: his plungers were of no use in fighting this blob, and he had just made the Crazy Clay really, *really* angry.

"**UH-OH,**" he said as he retracted his plunger ears, now covered in blue Crazy Clay glop.

The World's Biggest Lump of Crazy Clay lunged at him. Larryboy had to think quickly (which is not exactly his specialty). He grabbed a tennis racquet from a shelf and shouted, "**STAY BACK!**" while waving it at the blue blob.

The World's Biggest Lump of Crazy Clay simply seized the racquet and absorbed it into his blue Crazy Clay body.

Next, Larryboy grabbed a paddleball and tried to intimidate the blob with the **BAPPITY-BAPPITY-BAPPITY** sound of the bouncing ball. But the blob snatched the paddleball and absorbed that too.

Larryboy looked around and grabbed a Miss Pretty Pretty doll. He held the doll out and said (in a doll's voice), "Hi! I'm Miss Pretty Pretty. I am so cute. La la la la la! Please don't smash me all to bits, Mr. Blue Crazy Clay Monster! La la la la la!"

Unimpressed, The World's Biggest Lump of Crazy Clay absorbed Miss Pretty Pretty too. (It seemed the cute little dolly routine didn't work on crazed monsters.) Then the Crazy Clay grabbed Larryboy and picked him up off the ground. It looked like Larryboy would be next!

"Hey," said Larryboy. "I've got an idea. How about you and I play a game of badminton? Doesn't that sound like fun?"

Apparently it did not sound like fun to the Crazy Clay.

What apparently *did* sound like fun to the Crazy Clay was to pick up Larryboy and throw *him* to the ground, and that's what it did. Larryboy looked around desperately, grabbing the only thing he could reach…a toy saxophone.

"A toy saxophone?" he shrieked as the Crazy Clay picked him up again. "Why don't they design toys with monster-destroying capabilities?"

Larryboy would have preferred to develop a new plan of attack at that point. However, he was about to be absorbed by The World's Biggest Lump of Crazy Clay, so he did the only thing he could think of. He closed his eyes, blew a long soulful note on the saxophone, and waited to be absorbed.

CHAPTER 4

CLAYMOTION

To Larryboy's great surprise, when he opened his eyes, he had not been absorbed. In fact, The World's Biggest Lump of Crazy Clay set him down and began rocking back and forth to the music.

"Hey! I wasn't absorbed!" said Larryboy. He was so surprised that he stopped saxophoning.

Then the blob stopped swaying and smashed a model train.

"Larryboy!" shouted Archie, who had just made his way into the store. "The Crazy Clay blob seems to *like* the saxophone! Keep playing!"

"What should I play?" asked Larryboy as the blob moved toward him in a way that indicated that more smashing was about to occur.

"Anything!" shouted Archie. "Play anything!"

So Larryboy played the first thing that came into his head, which happened to be "The Song of the Cebu." Once again the Crazy Clay stopped smashing stuff and started swaying to the music. The World's Biggest Lump of Crazy Clay was...*dancing!* It danced the twist, the hustle, and the mashed potato. That Crazy Clay could really rock and roll!

After a few moments of dancing, Larryboy got a great idea. He started playing a lullaby, and before long The World's Biggest Lump of Crazy Clay was sound asleep.

Soon after that, the zookeeper from the Bumblyburg City Zoo arrived to take the sleeping Crazy Clay away.

"AWWW," said Larryboy, looking at the dozing Crazy Clay. "That horrible monster almost killed me, but the Crazy Clay looks so cute when it's sleeping. It was probably just cranky because it needed a nap."

"Well, don't worry, Larryboy," said the zookeeper. "We'll give it a nice home...in a glass cage where it can't ooze through the bars and escape."

"That's a good idea," said Larryboy.

As the zookeeper drove away, Archie hopped up beside Larryboy. "My, my," he said. "That was quite a lot of excitement for a day that started out with standing in line for Hula Heidi."

"Hula Heidi!" exclaimed Larryboy. "I almost forgot!"

Larryboy dove under the pile of stuffed animals again, changed out of his Larryboy costume, and raced to the Hula Friends section.

When he got there, he heard some horrible news.

"Sorry," said Mr. Snappy. "All of the Hula Heidis are gone."

"Oh no!" said Larry. "How can this be?"

"Someone came in and bought up every last Hula Heidi doll," said Mr. Snappy. "Maybe you'd like a slightly smashed model train instead...at a discount?"

"OH, HULA HEIDI!" cried Larry. **"WHY? WHY? WHY??** Why did you let someone buy every last one of you?"

CHAPTER 5

PUDDLE, PUDDLE, MUDDY TROUBLE

Larry went home feeling quite disappointed and turned on all of his lawn sprinklers so he would have mud puddles to jump in. He always jumped in mud puddles when he was upset. Today, Larryboy was *very* upset...and *ve-e-ery* muddy. Archie chased Larry around with a towel, trying to wipe him clean. But Larry just splashed Archie with mud too. If Archie didn't cheer up Larry soon, neither one of them would be clean enough to go into the house!

"But Master Larry! Think of all the Hula Friends you already have!" said Archie looking at all of Larry's Hula Friends he had been pulling along in a little red wagon. The Hula Friends were dancing cheerfully to the rhythm of the islands. Larry looked at them, but it didn't cheer him up.

"Look at Hula Hank!" said Archie. "See his cute little ukulele. Isn't he cutesy-wootsy?"

"Take them away! They're mocking me! I know what they're thinking behind their pleasant Hawaiian smiles! They're thinking, **YOU DON'T HAVE HULA HEIDI! YOU DON'T HAVE US ALL!** That's what they're *really* thinking! They're

thinking it so loud, I can even hear them! I'm incomplete! In-com-plete!"

Archie was beginning to worry about Larry. He knew it wouldn't really make Larry happy even if he could get the latest Hula Friend. But obviously, Larry had not learned that lesson yet. So Archie decided that maybe the best thing to do would be to get his friend's mind off of Hula Heidi.

"Well, Master Larry, you can just keep on jumping in mud puddles, but I'm going to go get ready."

"Ready for what?" asked Larry.

"Have you forgotten? Tonight is the first night of the *Bumblyburg Yodeling Festival*! And...I recently found out that world-famous yodeler Einger Warblethroat III is performing!"

"Einger Warblethroat III?" shouted Larry. "He is my very favorite yodeler of all time! He's the only one in the world who can yodel and play the accordion at the same time!"

Archie's strategy worked. Larry forgot all about Hula Heidi. He started hopping back to the mansion where he could get ready for the concert. Archie hopped after him. "Larry, don't track mud all over the floor," he called.

CHAPTER 6

EINGER WARBLETHROAT III

Larry, Archie, and everyone else in Bumblyburg gathered at the Bumblyburg Music Hall for the opening night of the *Bumblyburg Yodeling Festival*. Everyone in Bumblyburg was excited; they *loved* yodeling. In fact, they loved yodeling even more than they loved mud wrestling!

Mayor Fleming hopped up onto the stage. "Good evening friends! Let's give a great big warble welcome to Einger Warblethroat III!"

The citizens of Bumblyburg cheered loudly as Einger Warblethroat III made his way onstage with his accordion. Larry cheered loudest of all.

Einger began yodeling, **"YODEEL-EEIDEY-IDDEY-EEIDY. YODEEL-EEIDEY-IDDEY-EEIDY. YODEEL-EEI-DEY-IDDEY-EEIDY-OOO."** (It was a famous

yodeling song about a two-headed yak and his favorite lollipop.)

Then, right in the middle of the yodeling, there was another sound, a sound that didn't sound like yodeling at all. It sounded a lot like someone was tearing a hole in the roof. And, as a matter of fact, that was exactly what was happening.

Larry and everyone else watched as a glass tube extended through the hole in the roof. Down, down it came and **WHOOSH!** It sucked Einger Warblethroat III and his accordion right through the roof with a little **PFFFT** sound.

Everyone applauded wildly.

"Yea!" shouted Larry. "That Einger Warblethroat III sure knows how to put on a great show!"

Mayor Fleming dashed onstage and yelled, "Walloping

Warblethroat! Citizens of Bumblyburg, that was not part of the show! Einger Warblethroat III has been...*yodelnapped!*"

The audience gasped.

"Is there a hero in the house?" asked Mayor Fleming. Larry realized that once again, **I...AM...THAT...HERO!**

He leaped to his feet and shouted, **"I AM..."**

"Larry!" Archie whispered with a nudge. "Don't give away your secret identity!"

"Oh yeah. I forgot," Larry whispered back.

"Yes, Larry?" said Mayor Fleming. "Did you have something you wanted to say?"

Larry realized that everyone was now looking at him. He tried to think quickly. "I am...I am...um...I am going to go to the bathroom!"

He rushed out the door and headed to the bathroom, "Whew! That was close. But telling them I was on the way to the bathroom was a really smart thing to do."

Archie shrugged nervously. "When you gotta go, you gotta go."

Moments later it was Larryboy who rushed into the music hall. **"I...AM...THAT...HERO!"**

"Larryboy!" said Mayor Fleming. "How warbly wonderful!

We're mighty glad to see you! Einger Warblethroat III has been whisked away!"

"Don't worry, Mayor. Larryboy is on the case!" said Larryboy. "Plungers away!"

He shot his plunger ears up through the hole in the roof and pulled himself upwards. Unfortunately he kinda missed the hole and ended up bonking his head on the ceiling.

"I'm OK!" he said as he dangled from his plunger cords. Again he tried to flip himself up through the hole, but he was a little woozy from hitting his head and only succeeded in smacking his face against the ceiling.

Archie winced. "I'm still OK!" said Larryboy. Finally he managed to pull himself up so that his nose stuck through the hole. Then he used his nose to pull the rest of his body through just in time to see a helicopter flying away. He could see Einger's face pressed against the window.

Larryboy launched a plunger at the helicopter, but it was too far away to reach. Larryboy had no way to chase them. His Larryplane was back at the Larrycave.

As he helplessly watched the helicopter fly away, he faintly heard Einger cry, **"HEEEELLLP-EE-HEEDY-HOODDY-OOODY HEELLLP-EE-OOODY-OO!"**

CHAPTER 7

GREEDY GRETA AND THE PUDDING GLOP

Later that night, Einger Warblethroat III
found himself inside a glass tube in a room in a
deep, deep, sub-, sub-basement of a large castle.
He looked around and said, "Would you look at
that!" All of the rest of the world's greatest yodelers
were there too, and they were also trapped inside
glass tubes.

About now you may be thinking, *Who could be so
rotten and villainous as to yodelnap all of the world's
greatest yodelers and deprive the citizens of
Bumblyburg, as well as the rest of the world, of
quality yodeling entertainment? Who would be so
greedy as to only think of his or her own yodeling needs?*

Well, as it so happened, Einger
Warblethroat III had those very same
questions on

his mind. "Who would ever do such a confounded crazy thing?" he cried.

Suddenly, an easy chair in the center of the room swung around toward him. In it sat a green zucchini wearing a jewel-encrusted tiara and a pearl necklace. "I would," she said.

"And just who might *you* be?" asked Einger.

"I am Greedy Greta, the greedy zucchini," she said.

Greedy Greta lived in a castle in a mountainous alpine village just outside Bumblyburg. Her uncle Green Gregor, the gruesome zucchini, had given her the castle. Green Gregor had made his fortune selling rare bottle caps. He had collected them when he was just a wee zucchini and had passed all of his great wealth to Greedy Greta as an inheritance. Now Greedy Greta had more money than she knew how to spend. But did her money make her happy? It did not!

So Greta decided maybe she would be happy if she bought whatever she wanted. This, however, didn't make her happy either. Then she realized that there were some things that even she didn't have enough money to buy. So she began to steal things. But that didn't make her happy

either. Still she kept trying. She was convinced that if she just had a few more things, she would finally attain true happiness.

But why would she yodelnap all of the world's greatest yodelers? Einger Warblethroat III had that very same question, so he asked, "Why would you yodelnap all of the world's greatest yodelers?"

"I *love* yodeling!" said Greedy Greta.

"Yeah, but so does everyone else!" said Einger.

Greedy Greta got up from her easy chair at the center of the room and made her way over to Einger. "I listened

to yodeling concerts and I listened to the CDs, but that wasn't enough for me! I wanted *more* yodeling! So I decided I would kidnap a yodeler so that I could make him yodel whenever I wanted."

"That's pretty greedy," said Einger.

"But then I realized that I wasn't happy with just one yodeler. If I was going to be happy, I would have to yodelnap **ALL** of the world's greatest yodelers for myself. That way I could have them at my beck and call for my own private yodeling concert whenever I wished!"

"But there's one thing you didn't think about," said

Einger. "I won't yodel for you! I *never* perform for yodel-nappers!"

"Oh, I think you will!" said Greedy Greta as she sat back down in her easy chair. "If you don't, I will press this button right here."

"I won't," insisted Einger.

So Greta pressed the button on the side of her chair, and a glop of smelt-flavored pudding fell onto Einger's head.

"EEEEWW!" said Einger. "Smelt-flavored pudding!"

"Our family recipe!" beamed Greta.

CHAPTER 8

MOPPING THINGS UP

The next day, Larry rode the elevator up to the offices of the *Daily Bumble* newspaper where he worked as a janitor. He didn't really enjoy working as a janitor. He didn't need the money. He already had a mansion and a butler. Besides, being a janitor involved *way* too much mopping, at least that's what Larry thought.

He only took the job at the *Daily Bumble,* so he could eavesdrop on the reporters. Then he'd be the first to know when there was trouble that needed to be handled by Larryboy.

As the elevator climbed to the top floor, Larry's mop rang.

That's right, his mop rang.

Archie had installed a hi-tech feature in

Larry's mop so that he and Larry could talk with each other whenever they needed to.

Everyone in the elevator looked at the funny janitor with the ringing mop. Larry threw the wet end of the mop over his head. This wasn't just to avoid the funny looks he was getting. Throwing the mop over his head was the way he activated the video screen that let him communicate with Archie.

"How are you doing, Master Larry?" asked Archie, as the image of his face appeared on the mop video screen.

"I'm on the elevator, just about to report for work,"

replied Larry.

"What? But, Larry, you left for work more than an hour ago!"

"I know, but I stopped for a jelly doughnut," said Larry.

Archie sighed. "Oh well," he said. "Listen, Larry, we need to find out as much information as we can about the yodelnapper. So if any of the reporters at the *Daily Bumble* have any news, hold your mop up to his or her mouth."

"EEEEW! Why would I want to do that?" asked Larry.

"Because the microphone in your mop will transmit the information to me, and then we can analyze the data in the Larrycomputer," said Archie.

"OK, over and out!" said Larry as the doors of the elevator opened. Larry tried to hop out of the elevator, but the mop was still draped over his head and he tripped. Before Larry could get up, the elevator doors closed on his head.

"OWWWWIEEEE!" yelled Larry.

"Are you OK?" asked a voice nearby.

Larry pulled the mop off of his head and looked up to see Vicki Cucumber, the photographer for the *Daily Bumble*, looking down at him. *Oh no!* thought Larry. *Why does Vicki, the most beautiful cucumber in all of Bumblyburg, always show up when I'm in the most embarrassing positions?*

"Oh, yeah, I'm fine." he said nervously.

"Then why are you lying on the floor, letting the elevator doors close on your head?" Vicki asked.

"Well, you see, as a janitor, I have to look for dirt from every angle! Dirt can be sneaky! And grime! Grime is good at hiding in the elevator doors. Sometimes I have to get down and look real close!"

"Well, Larry, that's really…fascinating. But I have to

run. We're having a big meeting about the yodelnapper story. Bye!" She hopped away quickly.

Larry felt really silly, and he wanted to run away and hide. But he knew that he had to see what information he could get about the yodelnapper, so he—hopped over to where the staff was talking.

"I want all available reporters to see what they can find out about the yodelnapping." said Bob. "This is the biggest story in Bumblyburg since the mayor accidentally glued his moustache to the garbage truck!"

"I hear this yodelnapping goes deeper than just the *Bumblyburg Yodeling Festival*," said Vicki.

"Yeah," chimed in rookie reporter Junior Asparagus. "Yodelers are disappearing from all over the world!"

Larry stuck his mop right in Junior's face. "Um…could you repeat that?"

"Yodelers are disappearing from all over the world," said Junior, trying to brush the stray mop strands out of his nose.

"OH NO!" said Larry. "Who could be doing such dastardly deeds?"

"No one knows," said Vicki. Larryboy quickly shoved

the mop in her face. "All the usual supervillains like Awful Alvin, the Alchemist, and the Emperor and Lampy are already behind bars."

"Looks like we've got a new supervillain out there," said Junior.

"A dastardly new yodelnapping supervillian on the loose!" said Bob. "Hey…that sounds like a good headline! Larry! What are you doing?" he asked as Larry jabbed the mop in front of Bob's face.

"Oh, um, I…uh…I thought I saw some grime on your face, and I thought I should mop it up," Larry explained as he wiped Bob's face with the mop.

"Larry!" growled Bob with a scowl.

"Sorry." Larry quickly moved the mop a little farther away.

"Don't ever mop me up again, unless I specifically ask you to!" snapped Bob, hopping away angrily. But moments later he returned. "Well, what are all of you waiting for?" he shouted to his reporters. "This story isn't going to report itself!"

The news staff scattered, eager to get the big story. And Larry was left standing alone with his mop.

Just then the mop rang, so Larry threw it over his head.

"Did you get all of that?" Larry asked the video image of Archie.

"Yes, but I'm afraid this case is worse than we thought! We don't even know who the yodelnapper is!" exclaimed Archie.

"What are we going to do?" asked Larry.

"I don't know," said Archie. "Maybe you should ask Bok Choy's advice when you get to superhero class tonight."

CHAPTER 9

SOB CHOY

Bok Choy stood at the front of the class, crying like a big baby chicken that just lost his favorite pair of red rubber galoshes.

Larryboy and the other superheroes had never seen their teacher like that before. Quite frankly they were worried about him.

"I can't believe he's gone!" sobbed Bok Choy. "Why would someone yodelnap Einger Warblethroat III? Why, why, why?"

Einger Warblethroat III was Bok Choy's favorite yodeler. He liked to listen to Einger's CDs every morning as he did his superhero exercises.

But now Einger was gone and Bok Choy was taking it really hard.

"Are you OK, sir?" asked Electro Melon.

Bok Choy tried to compose himself. "Yes," he said. "Yes, please forgive me. I'm going through a tough time. But as an ex-superhero, I must remember that I've faced tougher challenges than this." He took a deep breath before continuing. "So, let's get to tonight's lesson, shall we? Tonight, I want to tell you heroes about the dangers of materialism."

Larryboy leaned over to Dark Crow, a grape who wished he wasn't vegetable. If anyone could judge Bok

Choy's disposition, it was him. "You think he's going to be all right?" Larryboy asked.

"I don't know," said Dark Crow. "Warblethroat was Master Choy's favorite."

"I hope he's OK. I was gonna ask him for some advice after class."

"I'm OK now," continued Bok Choy, blowing his nose. "Okeydokey. A hero should not base his happiness on material things," said Bok Choy. "Can anyone give me an example of a material thing?"

"Money!" said Lemon Twister.

"A fancy utility belt," Scarlet Tomato chimed in.

"A supersonic stealth plane," added Dark Crow.

"Good! Good! Any more?"

"The complete works of Enger Warblethroat III on CD?" asked Larryboy.

Bok Choy broke down sobbing again. "Oh, my poor Einger! My poor, poor Einger! Come back! Come back, Einger!"

"What?" asked Larryboy as everyone turned to look at him.

"Um…sir, would you like to take a break for a few minutes?" asked Lemon Twister.

"No," said Bok Choy. "I will finish the lesson. Ahem. If all you want in life is more material things, you will never feel like you have enough. You will never be satisfied. You will always want more and more, and this will make you miserable! To find lasting happiness, it is better to focus on the important things, like thinking more about others than you do about yourself. That's what will bring you lasting happiness."

Bok Choy took a moment to blow his nose.

"Turn in your superhero handbooks to section 21, paragraph 5, subsection 10. 'Whoever loves money never has money enough; whoever loves wealth is never satisfied with his income.' Think well upon this lesson. Are there any questions?"

"Yeah," said Larryboy. "I have a question about the supervillain who yodelnapped Einger Warblethroat the Thi..."

Bok Choy let out a wail of despair. "Einger! Einger! Einger! I want my Warblethroat!" He began beating his head against his desk.

"Um...never mind," said Larryboy.

CHAPTER 10

LEDERHOSEN!

That evening Larryboy went back to the Larrycave.

"So, did Bok Choy have any good ideas on how to catch the yodelnapper?" asked Archie.

"Well…no."

"I see," said Archie. "Oh well, no matter. I came up with a splendid plan all by myself!"

"That's great!" said Larryboy excitedly. "What is it? Tell me, tell me! What's the plan? Tell me the plan!"

Minutes later Larryboy hopped out from the Larryboy special-disguises changing room. Only he didn't look so much like Larryboy anymore. He was now wearing lederhosen and a wooden shoe over his Larryboy costume. A fake mustache and fake glasses worn over his mask complemented the lederhosen. In addition, he was pulling a life-sized toy sheep alongside himself.

"This is the plan?" asked a confused and embarrassed Larryboy.

"Well, yes," explained Archie. "It's *part* of the plan. See, you're going to pose as a famous yodeler named Noodle Blabberbop."

"Ooh! I like the name! Blabberbop. It's fun to say. Blabberbop! Blabberbop! Blabberbop!" said Larryboy.

"Then, as Noodle Blabberbop, you will perform at the *Bumblyburg Music Festival.*"

"But what if the yodelnapper shows up?" asked Larryboy.

"Then you'll be yodelnapped!"

"But Archie, I don't *want* to be yodelnapped!" said Larryboy.

"Don't worry, Larryboy," said Archie. "It's all part of the plan. You're the bait for our trap. You will let the yodelnapper take you to where the other yodelers are being held. Then, you will escape with the help of some wonderful gadgets I've installed in this toy sheep. Once you escape, you can free the yodelers and capture the yodelnapper! Do you understand the plan?"

"Blabberbop! Blabberbop! Blabberbop!" Larryboy exclaimed gleefully.

"OK then. The first thing we have to do is to make sure that the yodelnapper knows about your upcoming performance."

"Did you say 'performance'?" asked Larryboy.

CHAPTER 11

BLABBERBOP BLABS TO THE *BUMBLE*

The next day, "Noodle Blabberbop" (and his toy sheep) held a press conference at the offices of the *Daily Bumble* to announce that he would be performing at the Bumblyburg Music Hall.

Everyone at the *Daily Bumble* was excited by the news. Everyone except Bob, that is. Bob was annoyed that the floors hadn't been mopped because Larry the janitor hadn't shown up for work yet.

"That's right," said Larryb...um...Noodle. "My appearance at the Music Hall will prove to everyone that I am truly the world's best yodeler!"

"If you're the world's best yodeler, how come we've never heard of you?" asked Junior Asparagus.

"Well...um...that's

because I've spent the last seven years in...outer space. Yeah! I've been the yodeling ambassador to Jupiter!"

"OOOOH!" said Junior. "I've always wanted to go to Jupiter! What are the aliens from Jupiter like?"

"Um...no more questions about Jupiter," said Noodle. "I was an ambassador *and* a spy! It was all very, very *top secret*," he added. Larryboy didn't like having to pretend he was someone else. It made him very uncomfortable.

Vicki took a picture of Noodle as the other reporters continued to ask him questions. She leaned toward Junior and whispered, "Does Noodle look familiar to you?"

"No, why?" asked Junior.

"I don't know. There's just something about him. I think he's kinda cute!" said Vicki with that look on her face that she normally only got when Larryboy was around. Junior just rolled his eyes.

"Please take plenty of pictures!" said Noodle. "I want to be on the front page, so that *everyone* will know about my performance!"

"I think we can put you on the front page," said Editor Bob. "Unless there's a bigger story today... like a story about all the horrible things I'm gonna do to our janitor

when he finally shows up!"

Noodle gulped nervously.

"Noodle, one more question," said Junior. "Aren't you afraid of the yodelnapper?"

"Absolutely not!" said Noodle. "Just let that yodelnapper *try* to nab me! I'm not the least little itty-bitty bit afraid!"

CHAPTER 12

GREEDY GRETA GETS GRATUITOUSLY GREEDY

Back at Greedy Greta's castle, Greta sat down in her easy chair with fourteen copies of the *Daily Bumble*.

"Why do you have so many copies?" asked Einger, who was still trapped inside his glass tube.

"I have never been satisfied with just one copy of the paper," said Greedy Greta. "So I follow the paperboy around every morning and take papers from my neighbors' porches. But I always leave each neighbor a quarter for them."

"That sounds frightfully greedy!" said Einger.

"Quiet down and yodel for me while I read my paper, Yodelboy!"

Einger, not wanting smelt-flavored pudding dumped onto his head again, began yodeling vigorously as Greta began reading the *Daily Bumble*.

As she looked at the front page, she couldn't help but see the picture of Noodle Blabberbop.

"What's this?" cried Greedy Greta. "Another yodeler? This means there's a yodeler out there that I don't have! And he says he's the greatest yodeler in the world!"

"But Greta," said Einger. "Don't you think…"

"Who told you to stop yodeling?" she shrieked. She

was so angry about not having *all* of the world's best yodelers that she pressed the button on her chair and dropped smelt-flavored pudding onto the heads of all the yodelers.

"This Noodle Blabberbop says he's not the least little itty-bitty bit afraid of being yodelnapped. Well, we'll just see about that!"

CHAPTER 13

ARCHIE'S PLAN GETS A LITTLE CLOGGED

The next day, Noodle Blabberbop and Archie stood behind the stage curtain of the Bumblyburg Music Hall. "Well, this is it." said Archie. "Your big performance!"

Mayor Fleming appeared onstage. "I'm so excited, I just want to blabber on and on about it! Let me introduce to you Noodle Blabberbop and his toy sheep!"

Everyone applauded as Noodle hopped from behind the stage curtain, wearing his lederhosen and wooden shoe. He hopped toward the front of the stage, pulling his toy sheep. But then, suddenly, he stopped. His eyes opened wide with panic.

Everyone in Bumblyburg was there...and looking right at *him*.

He darted back behind the curtain.

Archie rushed up to him.

"Larrybo…um…I mean Noodle, what's wrong? You have to go back onstage!"

"But…but…everyone's out there. Bob, Junior…*Vicki*! They were all *watching* me!"

"Of course," said Archie. "They came to hear you yodel."

"But Archie, I just remembered something," said Noodle. "I don't know *how* to yodel!"

"You don't have to yodel," said Archie. "The yodelnapper will yodelnap you."

"But what if he doesn't show up?" asked Noodle.

"Don't worry! The yodelnapper *will* show up. Now you get back out there!" said Archie as he shoved Noodle back onstage.

There was another brief moment of applause, followed by complete silence. Noodle looked out at the crowd. They looked back.

No yodelnapper.

"So...um...nice weather we're having, huh?" said Noodle nervously.

The crowd looked back at him. Still no yodelnapper.

"Hey!" said Noodle. "Did you hear the one about the one-eyed pirate and the cantaloupe?"

Someone from the back of the music hall yelled, "Yodel already!"

Noodle knew he couldn't stall any longer. The time had come...to fake it.

"YODEL YODEL YODEL YODEL YODEL YODEL YODEL YODEL YODEL YODEL," sang Noodle.

The crowd began to frown. "He's not even yodeling!" said Bob.

"Yeah, he's just singing the word 'yodel' over and over," said Junior.

The crowd began to boo. Noodle began to sweat. And lederhosen are not very comfortable once you start to sweat in them! *Where is that yodelnapper?*

The booing got louder. *I gotta do something*, Noodle realized.

And so, out of desperation, Noodle did the only thing he could think of doing. He began clog dancing.

CLOPPITY-CLOPPITY went his one wooden shoe.

The crowd stopped booing. In fact they started cheering instead. Apparently the citizens of Bumblyburg loved clog dancing almost as much as they loved yodeling!

As the cheering increased, Noodle began to enjoy himself. *They love my dancing! They love me! I've clogged my way into their hearts!*

But, just as Noodle was beginning to envision a clogging world tour, a glass tube crashed through the ceiling and sucked him and his toy sheep up into an awaiting helicopter.

He had been yodelnapped!

CHAPTER 14

LOTS OF SMELT-FLAVORED PUDDING

Greedy Greta stood Noodle inside the glass tube next to all the other yodelers.

"Finally," said Greedy Greta, "I have *all* of the world's greatest yodelers! Even the great yodel ambassador to Jupiter!"

"So, *you're* the yodelnapper!" exclaimed Noodle.

"That's right! I, Greedy Greta, the Greedy Zucchini, have yodelnapped all of the world's greatest yodelers to satisfy my need to have yodeling upon command!

"That's pretty greedy," said Noodle. "I mean, yodel-napping one yodeler is bad enough, but yodelnapping *all* of us?

"What's the point if you don't have the whole set?" she replied. "Now stop talking and yodel for me!"

"Um… I can't," he said.

"You'd better do it," said Einger from the next tube. "You don't want to make her mad."

"Sorry, but I can't," said Noodle.

"Wrong answer!" said Greedy Greta as she pressed the button and dumped smelt-flavored pudding onto his head.

"EEEECH! I got pudding down my lederhosen!" yelped Noodle.

"Yodel, Noodle! Yodel!" Greta demanded.

"Well, the truth is, I don't know how," said Noodle.

"Wrong answer!" said Greedy Greta as more smelt-flavored pudding fell onto Noodle's head.

"Just give me a second to explain!" said Noodle. "Besides, I really hate having smelt-flavored pudding dumped onto my head."

"I know! Everyone does! Now, are you going to yodel or do you want another dose?" asked Greta.

"I can't yodel because…"

SPLAT. Another glob of smelt-flavored pudding fell onto his head.

"Wait! Let me explain!" begged Noodle.

SPLAT!

"I can do this all day!" said Greedy Greta. "I've got a whole lot of pudding!"

"But I really don't know how to yodel," said Noodle.

"That's absurd! How can you be a world-famous yodeler if you don't know how to yodel?" asked Greedy Greta.

"Because I'm not really a world-famous yodeler," said Noodle. At that moment, he ripped off his Noodle disguise, revealing his true identity. **"I...AM...THAT...HERO!"**

"Larryboy!" exclaimed a shocked Greedy Greta. "I didn't know you could yodel."

"I can't," said Larryboy. "I came to save the yodelers!"

"HOORAY-EEDI-EEIDI-OOODLE-IIEDY-YAY-YAY!" cheered the yodelers.

"I demand that you release me and the yodelers this instant!" said Larryboy.

"No!" said Greedy Greta.

"Oh," said Larryboy.

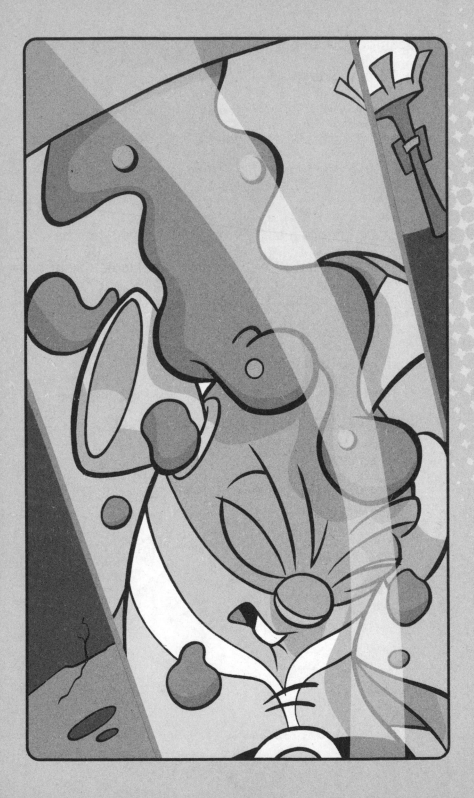

CHAPTER 15

THE HARD WAY

This was disappointing for Larryboy. He had

hoped that Greedy Greta would just sorta give up,

let everyone go, and turn from her wicked ways. But

it looked like he'd have to do things the hard way.

"OK, Greedy Greta, you give me no choice."

"And you give me no choice but to dump even *more*

pudding onto your head!"

She dumped more pudding onto his head.

"Now cut that out!"

Then she dumped more pudding onto his head.

"That's really starting to get annoy… "

She dumped even *more* pudding onto his head!

At that point, Larryboy decided that maybe

he'd better just shut his big mouth before

the whole glass tube, in which he

was still trapped,

would be filled with smelt-flavored pudding. He also decided that it was time to activate the escape mechanism Archie had installed inside the toy sheep.

Larryboy fired his plunger ears at the sheep. When he retracted them, each ear was plugged with sheep wool. Then he pressed a button on the sheep labeled **PRESS TO ESCAPE.**

The sheep gave out a high-pitched **"BAAAAA!"** causing the glass tube holding Larryboy to break open. Greta quickly hopped out of the way.

Unfortunately for Larryboy, when the tube broke open, all of the pudding inside it carried him along like a smelt-flavored tidal wave. Finally Larryboy came to a stop and stood up, covered in even more smelt-flavored pudding.

"YUCKY!" he said.

Luckily Archie had installed some other special equipment inside the toy sheep. Larryboy pushed another button and a robotic arm holding a squeegee came out of the sheep's back and wiped Larryboy clean.

"Thanks, toy sheep!" said Larryboy.

"BAAAA," said the toy sheep, but Larryboy didn't hear him. He still had wool in his ears.

"Now it's time to free the yodelers!" said Larryboy. He hopped over to a panel labeled **YODELER'S RELEASE.** He pulled a lever and the glass tubes holding the yodelers sank into the floor, and the yodelers were free.

"YAAAY-YAY-YAY-EEIDY-IIEDY-EEIDY-OOO!" cheered the yodelers.

"You'll never get away with this, Larryboy!" cried Greta.

"What?" asked Larryboy. "Hold on a second." He removed the wool that was still sticking out of his ears. "What did you say?"

"I said you'll never get away with this! I won't let you take my yodeler collection. How could I ever be happy without all of the world's best yodelers belonging only to me? If I don't have them all, I'll never be satisfied!"

"You know," said Larryboy, "this reminds me of something my superhero instructor, Bok Choy, said in class the other day: 'Whosoever loves money never has money enough; whoever loves wealth is never satisfied with his income.'"

"What's that supposed to mean?" sneered Greedy Greta.

"It means that if all you want in life is to gain material

things like money or supersonic jets or really cool plungers or..."

"Or all of the world's best yodelers," added Einger.

"Right! If you base your happiness on material things, you'll never feel like you have enough. You'll never be satisfied, and that will make you miserable," said Larryboy.

"If you think your little speech is going to get me to give up my collection, then I think you're wearing your plungers too tight!" said Greedy Greta.

As she said this, she flipped a switch that opened a trapdoor in the floor underneath Larryboy and the other yodelers.

"AAAAAAAUGH!" said Larryboy as he and the yodelers fell into a dark room.

"Just a minute," said Larryboy. "I have a flashlight in here somewhere."

Larryboy began pulling gadgets from his utility belt. He found a saw, an electric fan, a feather duster, a back scratcher, a mousetrap, but no flashlight.

"Hey," said Einger Warblethroat. "Do you hear something?"

Larryboy and the yodelers all listened in the darkness surrounding them. They *could* hear something. It seemed to be coming from the shadows.

Was it the sound of marching feet and...Hawaiian music?

CHAPTER 16

LARRYBOY COMPLETES HIS COLLECTION

Frightened, Larryboy and the yodelers stood close together. Finally Larryboy dug a little deeper and found his flashlight. He shined it around the dark room. In the light, they could see hundreds of dolls marching toward them.

"Oh boy! Hula Friends!" said Larryboy.

Greedy Greta looked down at them through the trapdoor.

"Meet *my* Hula Friends," she cackled.

"You like Hula Friends?" asked Larryboy.

"I'm a big fan of the Hula Friends! I even bought every last Hula Heidi at Mr. Snappy's Extremely Gigantic Toy Emporium."

"That was *you*?" asked Larryboy.

"That's right!" said Greta. "I can't get

enough Hula Friends! I buy as many as I can get, but I always want more and more! I've got quite a collection! But unfortunately for you, I've modified these Hula Friends to *attack*! You'll never escape from them! Attack! Attack, my hula minions!"

"What are we gonna **DOO-IEEDEE-OOH-OODY-OOODY-IIEDY-OOH?**" asked Einger.

"Well, I know what I'm going to do!" said Larryboy. "If Greedy Greta doesn't want those dolls any more, I'm gonna complete my Hula Friends collection!"

Larryboy shot out one of his plunger ears and snagged a Hula Heidi.

"Hula Heidi! At last, you are mine!" he said as the other Hula Friends continued to advance.

"But...but what about them?" asked Einger.

Larryboy turned and looked at the other Hula Friends. "You're right," he said. "Why have just one Hula Heidi when I could have one hundred!"

Larryboy rushed toward the other Hula Friends, but the yodelers jumped on top of him and held him down.

"What are you doing?" asked Larryboy. "All of the Hula Friends can be mine! I need more Hula Friends!"

"But Larryboy," said Einger, "don't you remember what your teacher said? If you base your happiness on getting more and more material things, you'll never feel like you have enough and you'll be miserable. If you can't think of anything but Hula Friends, you'll become just like Greedy Greta, the Greedy Zucchini!"

Larryboy thought about this for a moment and realized that what Einger said was true.

"You're right," said Larryboy. "I can't let myself become like her. She's a villain, and I...AM...THAT...HERO! I'm supposed to stop her!"

"Great," said Einger. "There's just one problem."

"What's that?" asked Larryboy.

Einger pointed to the ever-advancing Hula Friends who were practically upon them. "We're about to get hula-ed!"

The Hula Friends were getting ready to leap on top of Larryboy and the yodelers. "Stay back!" said Larryboy. "I'll handle this!"

Larryboy fought valiantly. He fired his plungers into the oncoming Hula swarm time and time again. But there were just too many of them. For every Hula doll he knocked down, there were dozens more to attack him with their ukuleles, their leis, and their enchanting island rhythms.

Soon they had wrestled him to the ground and were taking turns dancing on his head. "Hey! That hurts, you know!" said Larryboy. But the Hula Friends did not listen to Larryboy's cries for mercy. Greedy Greta had changed them from cute island dancers to vicious island meanies. Larryboy knew he had to retreat and come up with a new plan. He fired one of his plungers straight up, where it stuck to the ceiling. He then pulled himself up, shaking loose the Hula Friends that were still clinging to him. Finally he was free of the Hula Friends.

"Ha!" shouted Greedy Greta. "The yodelers are no match for my hula army!"

"There are too many of them!" Larryboy shouted to the yodelers.

"This looks like the end for us," sighed Einger as he played a sad little tune on his accordion.

"Einger! Your accordion!" Larryboy shouted down to Einger. "I just got a great idea! Do you know any polka music?"

"Sure," said Einger.

"Play a polka!" said Larryboy. "The Hula Friends may be Hawaiian, but no one can resist the crazy syncopation of a polka!"

Einger began playing a lively polka as the Hula Friends marched toward them.

Larryboy dropped back to the ground in front of the Hula dolls and began singing a song his Grampy Cucumber taught him years before: "The Purple Pickle Polka."

GO TO THE STORE AND BRUSH YOUR TEETH,
JUMP IN THE POOL WITH A CHRISTMAS WREATH,
AND THAT'S THE WAY WE DO, THE PURPLE PICKLE POLKA!

DRINK SOME SOAP AND FLY A KITE,
HOLD YOUR BREATH WITH ALL YOUR MIGHT,
AND THAT'S THE WAY WE DO, THE PURPLE PICKLE POLKA!

JUMP ON THE CHAIR WITH SHINY SHOES,
GO TO THE BEACH AND LOOK FOR CLUES.
BLINK YOUR EYES, CUSTARD PIES, PASTURIZE, DRAGON FLIES,
AND THAT'S THE WAY WE DO THE PURPLE PICKLE POLKA!
HEY! THAT'S THE WAY WE DO THE PURPLE PICKLE POLKA!

As Larryboy sang, the Hula Friends became confused.
They were made to hula...but they couldn't resist the
polka madness! They began to hop-step-close-step in
time with the music.

But their little joints weren't made for such lively
dancing. Soon their arms and legs began to spark, then
they began to give off smoke. They short-circuited and fell
over, broken.

"What have you done?" cried Greedy Greta. "You've
destroyed all of my beautiful Hula Friends!"

"I guess I just learned a lesson," replied Larryboy.
"Hula Friends are fun, and they're fun to play with. But

God wants us to remember that there are other, more important things than collecting material goods. And for me, one of those things is protecting Bumblyburg from villains like you!"

Larryboy launched one of his plunger ears up through the trapdoor and pulled himself up to the room where Greedy Greta was standing.

"YIKES," said Greedy Greta. She fled into an elevator, and the doors closed behind her. Larryboy watched as the lights on the elevator showed that Greta was going all the way to the top of the castle.

"Guess, I'll have to take the stairs," said Larryboy.

CHAPTER 17

THE SHEEP THAT BROKE THE HELICOPTER'S BACK

A few minutes later, Greedy Greta was on the castle's helicopter launching pad at the top of the castle, getting ready to escape. "Larryboy may have defeated my attack Hula Friends, but he'll never catch *me*! But if I have to escape, I'm going to take my things with me!" she cried.

Greta was loading everything she could into her helicopter. She had already loaded her bed, her bathtub, a set of potholders that looked like kittens, a toilet brush, a half-eaten doughnut, a ceramic statue of a poodle eating a marshmallow, all her lobster bibs, a giant swirly lollipop, a solar-powered waffle iron, twenty-four cases of gum, her blue fuzzy-bunny blanket, her salmon-flavored pillows, a jump

rope, seventy-six trombones, finger paints, her refrigerator magnet collection, the TV antenna, X-ray goggles, a broken hockey stick, a moldy lump of cheese, a throne, a partridge in a pear tree, and…well, just about everything else she owned too.

She just couldn't bear to leave anything behind.

"There," she said at last. "That's everything! I can keep all of my wonderful, wonderful stuff—and still escape!"

Just then Larryboy opened the stairway door and hopped outside, pulling the toy sheep behind him.

Exhausted from rushing up the stairs, he panted, "Who knew there could be so many stairs in a castle!"

Greedy Greta quickly started the helicopter. "There's no escape, Greedy Greta," said Larryboy.

But what Larryboy didn't know was that the helicopter was equipped with a smelt-flavored pudding squirter.

FWOOOSH!

A stream of yucky brown pudding knocked Larryboy backward. Greedy Greta began to take off. "Pudding won't save you this time!" said Larryboy as he hopped up and shot his plunger ears at the helicopter. But the plungers were covered with pudding and wouldn't stick. "Whadda you know," he said. "Maybe pudding *will* save you after all."

"You'll never catch me now!" said Greedy Greta.

Larryboy had to think fast. His plungers were useless. All at once he realized that he had a secret weapon to use against Greedy Greta: her own greediness!

"Greedy Greta," he shouted. "You left something behind. You might want it!"

"Something I might want?" she greedily shouting over the noise of the helicopter. "What is it? What could it be?"

Larryboy pulled the toy sheep from behind his back.

"My toy sheep. He's really cute!"

Greedy Greta grabbed a pair of binoculars and looked at the sheep. It gave a cute little **"BAAAA."**

"That toy sheep! I want it! I want that toy sheep," she shouted.

A glass tube extended down and sucked the sheep up into the helicopter.

"What a fabulous little sheep! How did I ever live without it? I love it! But...I'll need more toy sheep! One is not enough. I will need more! More sheep, I say!"

But then something happened. The helicopter began to tilt and rock. The addition of the toy sheep had made the helicopter too heavy to fly. Within moments the helicopter fell back down with a thud.

"Come on, you silly helicopter!" said Greedy Greta. But she was too greedy to lighten the load even one little bit, so the helicopter simply couldn't fly.

Larryboy hopped closer and shot a plunger ear at Greedy Greta, wrapping the plunger cord around and around her. "Sorry, Greedy Greta," said Larryboy, "but you're grounded."

CHAPTER 18

HOW ABOUT SOME MORE CLOG DANCING?

A few days later, with Greedy
Greta the Greedy Zucchini safely in jail,
Larryboy stood on stage at the Bumblyburg
Music Hall. The world's greatest yodelers in
their *Tribute to Larryboy* concert were serenading
him and the toy sheep.

Everyone applauded as the yodelers finished their
yodeling. Even Bob.

Einger hopped over and stood beside Larryboy.
"Larryboy, we want to thank you!" he said. "Without
you, the world would be deprived of quality yodeling
entertainment. Not only that, but all of us yodelers
would still be stuck inside glass tubes, fearing that
smelt-flavored pudding could be dropped onto our
heads at any second. Bumblyburg should be
proud to have such a hero!"

"I...AM...THAT...HERO!" said Larryboy.

"BAAAA," said the toy sheep.

The crowd applauded again. When the applause died down, Larryboy continued. "Thanks, everyone! I'm honored to serve and guard Bumblyburg against all crazy, dastardly foes! I learned something when fighting Greedy Greta, the Greedy Zucchini. You shouldn't base your happiness on material things. You'll just end up wanting more and more, and that will leave you so unhappy."

Vicki Cucumber sighed, "That Larryboy is just *so* cute!"

"Furthermore, I've decided to donate most of my collection of Hula Friends to kids who may not have their own. I realize now that I really don't need as many as I thought I did."

Backstage, Archie smiled. Larryboy truly had learned something.

"Now, since we're all here in the music hall, I wondered if everyone would like to hear me perform the polka song that defeated Greedy Greta? Hit it, Einger!"

Einger and the other yodelers surrounded Larryboy and began to pull him offstage. "Um, maybe not, Larryboy. I mean, last time you sang that song, you ended up short circuiting a whole army of toys!"

"OK. Well, how about some more clog dancing? Come on! I have worked up a brand-new number. You'll love it!"

"BAAAA," said the toy sheep.

THE END

VeggieTales

LarryBoy™

IN THE GOOD, THE BAD, AND THE EGGLY

WRITTEN BY
KENT REDEKER

ILLUSTRATED BY
MICHAEL MOORE

BASED ON THE HIT VIDEO SERIES: LARRYBOY
CREATED BY PHIL VISCHER
SERIES ADAPTED BY TOM BANCROFT

ZONDERkidz

ZONDERVAN.com/
AUTHORTRACKER
follow your favorite authors

TABLE OF CONTENTS

CHAPTER 1

FLYING THE SIZZLY SKIES

It was a peaceful night in the skies over Bumblyburg. The air was still with only the gentle flapping of passing pelicans to disturb the lazy clouds floating across the moon.

Not only were the skies peaceful, but they were safe, thanks to Bumblyburg's very own cucumber superhero...Larryboy!

Larryboy was spending the night doing routine patrols over Bumblyburg in his famous Larryplane. And since there was no crime or any other evil-doings afoot in the city tonight, all Larryboy had to do was sit back and relax. He was lucky enough to get a bird's eye view of the city that most of the citizens never got to see.

Some veggies would think that this was a wonderful chance to take in some of the natural beauty that God created.

But not Larryboy. Larryboy was bored.

"Archie!" he whined over the onboard communicator. "How much longer do I have to stay on patrol? There's not a single crime on the Larryscope! Nobody littering, nobody jaywalking, nobody wearing shoes that don't match their pants! Nothing! Why don't we just let police Chief Croswell handle things tonight?"

"But Larryboy," replied Archie, "as Bumblyburg's very own superhero, it's your duty to share the duties of protecting the city."

Archie was Larryboy's confidant, gadget-fixer, and closest friend. Plus, he was the butler of Larryboy's alter ego…Larry the Cucumber.

As such, he was also the only one who had to put up with Larryboy griping about patrol duty.

"But I don't want to share duties tonight! It's *boring*!" said Larryboy. "And boring rhymes with snoring, and snoring is what I do when I'm home in bed, which is where I'd rather be right now."

Archie frowned. He had tried to get Larryboy to take a nap this afternoon, but he wouldn't listen. Master Larry just *had* to stay up playing hopscotch. Archie knew that sharing didn't always seem like the most fun way to do things. But he also knew that in the end, God wants us to share!

"Hey, Archie! The lights are still on at *The Daily Bumble*," Larry said as he zoomed past the building where he worked undercover as the newspaper office janitor.

"Oh, it's just Bob putting the paper to bed," he said as he spied Vicki, the paper's renowned photojournalist. Larryboy smiled dreamily thinking that Vicki was truly the cutest "cuke" in town.

"You know, I think Vicki just might go to the Founder's

Day Party with you this year, if you'd get up the nerve to ask her," suggested Archie.

"Oh yeah, that'll happen, Arch. When pigs fly!" laughed Larryboy.

No sooner had Larryboy finished his sentence, when the Larryplane was attacked! Out of nowhere, three small supersonic objects zoomed past the Larryplane.

SPLAT! SPLAT! SPLAT! Three strips of bacon hit the windshield.

"Oh no! Bacon!" said Larryboy. "Archie, I've been *baconed*!!"

CHAPTER 2

PIGS ON THE WING

"Can you see who is attacking you?" asked Archie.

"Just a second," Larryboy answered as he turned on his windshield wipers to wipe off the greasy bacon while looking through the windshield to see his attackers. What he saw sent shivers through his cucumber body.

Archie had heard Larryboy say many strange things during their time together as crime fighters, but nothing prepared him for what he was about to hear.

"Archie!" said Larryboy. "Pigs *do* fly! I'm being attacked by flying pigs!"

Archie squinted at the images of the flying pigs that were being sent to him through the Larryplane's onboard cameras. While normally, pigs *can't* fly, these three little pigs were strapped into high-tech jet wings that had bacon cannons attached to each side.

"**OINK! OINK!**" came the sounds from the flying pigs.

"Why would flying pigs

shoot bacon?" asked Archie. "That doesn't make any sense!"

"Archie," said Larryboy, "could we think about that later? Right now I'd like to think about how to make them *stop* shooting bacon!"

The supersonic pigs were closing in...and fast. Larryboy made another quick turn, but this time the pigs stayed right behind him. "OK," said Archie. "The Larrycomputer has just given me some very interesting information. It seems that Willie, Wee-Wee, and Woozy, the three award winning pigs from the town of Maiseville,

were reported missing yesterday. Those pigs must be the pigs that are attacking you!"

Larryboy was about to tell Archie how useless he thought that information was, when another barrage of bacon hit one of the Larryplane's wings, causing the plane to spin out of control.

"AAAAAAH!" cried Larryboy as the plane plummeted towards the ground. "Archie! Something's wrong! I can't see!"

CHAPTER 3

AN EYE-OPENING EXPERIENCE

"Larryboy," said Archie, "open your eyes!"

Larryboy opened one eye, but he didn't like what he saw. The ground was getting closer and closer at an alarming rate. So Larryboy decided to close both eyes again.

Fortunately, Archie had installed a safety feature for just such an event. He had to because Larryboy had a tendency to close his eyes while flying the Larryplane. So, Archie pushed a button on the Larrycomputer and remotely activated the "Larryplane Automatic Anti-Closed-Eyes-Crash System", and the plane pulled up just in time to avoid a crash.

"Is it safe to look yet?" asked Larryboy.

"Yes, Larryboy, it's safe."

Larryboy opened his eyes. "Oh, that's better."

"Can you see where the pigs went?" Archie inquired.

"Yeah. They're not chasing me anymore! They're heading for downtown Bumblyburg."

"Downtown Bumblyburg!" exclaimed Archie. "Larryboy! You've got to stop them before they unleash their bacony assault upon the city!"

As Larryboy turned the Larryplane and raced off after the flying pigs, three dark figures on the ground below looked up to the sky and laughed at the exploits of our hero.

Well, two figures laughed at him. The other figure just sorta stood there.

Who would be so wicked as to chortle with glee in Larryboy's time of desperate need? It was none other than three of Larryboy's most archest-enemies of all: Greta Von Gruesome the Zucchini, Awful Alvin the Onion, and his sidekick, Lampy...the lamp.

"Ha ha!" cackled Awful Alvin. "My villainous plan of villainy is working to perfection!"

"*Your* plan?" said Greta. "You mean *my* plan to distract Larryboy so that no one will be able to stop us as we break into the Bumblyburg Science Labs!"

Lampy just stood there smiling. Lampy always smiled. That's one of the things Awful Alvin liked about him.

Awful Alvin was Bumblyburg's foremost evil genius. For some twisted reason, he just plain enjoyed being bad. He had a secret underground lair, and a burning desire to defeat Larryboy and rule Bumblyburg. Lampy was his faithful henchman. (Little is known about Lampy's background or family history.)

"I think that now is the time when we should perform the villainous dance of villainy to celebrate the villainous deeds we are about to perform!" said Awful Alvin. He grabbed Lampy. "Dance with me, Lampy!"

Greta rolled her eyes. She had agreed to be partners with Awful Alvin, but she wasn't sure it was worth it if

she had to put up with all his dancing and all around
oddities. After all, she owned a castle in the mountains
outside Bumblyburg. She owned everything she could
ever want...including silver-lined power gloves that fired
bolts of energy out of the brightly polished fingertips.

But, the fact was, Greta was really greedy, and even
with all her riches, she still wanted more! And she wanted revenge on Larryboy for all the times he had foiled her
plans to take more. With her and Awful Alvin's combined
villainous minds, they would finally be able to defeat
Larryboy once and for all. This time she was sure of it!

She just wished that Awful Alvin didn't feel the need
to do that silly dance all the time.

CHAPTER 4

LITTLE RED SCHNUGGLY-PUGGLY

The staff of *The Daily Bumble* was working late that night. It was hard at work providing Bumblyburg with up-to-date news every morning in time for their breakfast pastries and toast. Especially when there was a big, gigantic, spectacular story like there was today.

Bob the Tomato's mother was coming to Bumblyburg for a visit! This was big news!

Well, at least Bob thought it was. And since Bob was the editor of *The Daily Bumble,* his mom was front page news.

Bob hopped over to the desk where photographer, Vicki Cucumber, and cub reporter, Junior Asparagus, were working. "Here's a picture of my mom playing Parcheesi with a pigeon," he said. "Or, here's a picture of her juggling violins at the State Fair. Which do you think we should print on the front page?"

Vicki and Junior looked at each other. Bob loved his mother. All tomatoes do. But they thought it was a bit silly that the editor of a newspaper still allowed his mom to call him,

"My little red schnuggly-puggly!"

But before Vicki and Junior had a chance to respond, Bob saw something out the window.

"Hey!" he said. "Are those flying pigs?"

The flying pigs circled around. They had locked in *The Daily Bumble* building as the next target of their pork–products assault. They hovered midair as the compartments on their wings opened and large sausages emerged, ready to be fired.

Bob, Vicki, and Junior watched the pigs through the window, unaware of the danger they were in. Vicki began snapping pictures. Maybe, just maybe, she could convince Bob that a picture of flying pigs was more newsworthy than a picture of his juggling mother.

"Something's coming out of their wings," said Junior. "I think it's...it's...Polish sausages!"

Larryboy had also seen the meaty weapons emerge from the wings of the pigs. "Archie!" he said. "They're gonna shoot Polish Sausage Torpedoes at *The Daily Bumble*!"

"Oh dear me!" said Archie. "You have to find some way to stop them!"

"OINK! OINK!" went the pigs.

Then each of the pigs fired two sausage torpedoes, sending six meats of destruction right at Bob, Vicki, and Junior.

"Yikes!" howled Larryboy.

It was too late for clever planning or anything like that. So, Larryboy did the only thing he could do: he dove the Larryplane right into the path of the sausage.

HE IS THAT HERO!

The Larryplane took six direct hits of spicy meat. This was just too much for even the advanced circuitry of the Larryplane's Automatic Anti-Closed-Eyes-Crash System. The Larryplane spun out of control. It was all Larryboy could do to steer away from the large buildings. He decided to try and make a crash landing in the Bumblyburg City Park, since there probably wouldn't be anyone there at this time of night.

CHAPTER 5

A CRASH COURSE IN CRASHING

But, as the Larryplane lurched through the maze of buildings in downtown Bumblyburg, a solitary dark figure appeared atop a nearby building. This figure was not laughing (nor was he lamp-shaped, in case you were wondering.) The dark figure spread his cape and soared to the ground of the city park.

"Larryboy! Eject! Eject!" Archie shouted.

"I can't find the button!" said Larryboy. Archie had never thought to install an "Automatic-Eject-Larryboy-If-His-Eyes-Are-Closed-Again-System" to eject Larryboy by remote control.

"It's the blue button with the yellow star."

"I can't see it anywhere!" said Larryboy.

Larryboy's eyes were closed again.

"Open your eyes!" Archie told him.

Larryboy bravely peeked out from under his eyelids and whispered, **"I AM THAT HERO!"** as he fired both of his plunger ears, hitting a tree to each side of him. The ropes went taut and the plane plummeted to a bouncing halt, inches off the ground.

"WOW!" shouted Larryboy. "That was close!"

Larryboy released the ropes from his headpiece, and he and the plane dropped the last several inches to the ground.

"Larryboy, look out! The pigs are coming in for another attack!" shrieked Archie.

At that very moment, the dark figure shot out one of his talons from his belt and used it to swing across the sky. "Iyem…de Dark Crow!"

Who was this talon-bearing creature with a Spanish accent?

CHAPTER 6

SOMETHING TO CROW ABOUT

His name? Dark Crow.

He is a red grape that wears a black superhero costume that looks like a crow. He is the protector of the small, farming community of Maisefield. He is also a grape. But for some reason, Dark Crow doesn't like being a grape…that's why he took on the name Dark Crow. His crow-like supersuit and crow-like supergadgets give him a variety of ways to fight evildoers. Dark Crow takes crime-fighting *very* seriously. Larryboy knows him from the Superheroes Class at Bumblyburg Community College.

Dark Crow didn't think that Larryboy took super-heroing seriously enough. Not nearly seriously enough. But Larryboy was a superhero, none-the-less. And so, Dark Crow felt compelled to help one of his brothers in need.

"CA-CAW!"

"OINK! OINK!" the pigs called as Dark Crow swooped down in front of them.

The pigs veered to the side and circled around for another attack.

"Hello, Laddybuoy," said Dark Crow turning to face him. "Go home now. Get some rest, because theese case ees not big enough for the two of us."

"Huh?" said Larryboy who was oiling his ejector button with canola oil. "There! Good as new...ooops!"

The ejector seat fired and lunged Larryboy into the air. Fortunately for Dark Crow, Larryboy's ejector seat shot right into one of the flying pig's wings and smashed it all to bits.

With one wing ruined, the pig spun off and ricocheted into the other two flying pigs, ruining their wings as well. And without their hi-tech flying wings, the pigs weren't able to fly. They all fell with a **SPLASH** into Bumblyburg Park Lake.

Dark Crow rushed to the edge of the lake, pulled three small packets from his utility belt, and threw them to the pigs. The packets quickly inflated into black life-preservers with beaks and wings…just like a crow. The pigs grasped the life-preservers and floated to shore.

"Hey there, Dark Crow, good thing I ejected into those pigs. Otherwise, you might'a had a cowl full of bacon, huh?" asked Larryboy as he floated to the ground, thanks to the ejector seat's parachute. Unfortunately, the parachute got caught in a tree, and Larryboy was left dangling several feet from the ground.

"Are you kidding me? They never would haff snuck up on me eef I hadn't been busy saving you. They wouldn't stand a chance against…de Dark Crow!" Dark Crow said with a very Spanish accent and without a trace of friendliness in his voice.

Larryboy unhooked himself from his ejector seat and fell to the ground with an "Oof!" Then, he hopped after Dark Crow. "Well, thanks for saving me from the last pig attack. That was really…super."

"Look, Larryboy," Dark Crow scowled at him. "I saved you because eet's part of the superhero code. But why don't you just leave me alone now. You're messing up my case!"

"*Your* case?" asked Larryboy.

"That's right," said Dark Crow. "Awful Alvin and Greta Von Gruesome kidnapped those pigs from Maiseville yesterday, and I tracked them here to Bumblyburg."

"Greta Von Gruesome and Awful Alvin!" exclaimed Larryboy. "Lampy too?"

"Yes, Lampy too."

"Well, since they came to Bumblyburg, I can help you catch them!" said Larryboy with an excited smile on his face.

Dark Crow turned around angrily. He had no intentions of sharing his case with Larryboy, or anyone else for that matter. "I don't need any help! Just stay out of my way!"

"But...," said Larryboy as he was interrupted by the sound of Archie's voice coming over the communicator in his ear.

"Larryboy," said Archie, "an alarm has just gone off at the Bumblyburg Science Labs. Looks like a break-in. You better check it out."

"A break-in at the Bumblyburg Science Labs!" asked Larryboy.

Dark Crow spun back around as he heard this. "Egads! It must be Awful Alvin and Greta. Those flying peeegs were simply a big fat distraction to keep us *muy occupado* while they committed their villainous crimes! I haff to stop them!"

"Great!" Larryboy told him. "We can stop them together."

"Together? I giggle about this loudly in your peeekle juices!"

"I'm a cucumber!"

"De Dark Crow needs help from no-vegetable!" he said and was gone. He had disappeared into the night.

"Hey, wait up!" called Larryboy. "Could I catch a ride? My Larryplane's gonna be in the shop awhile!"

CHAPTER 7

THIS LITTLE LAMPY OF MINE

Dark Crow was right. Greta, Awful Alvin, and Lampy had broken into the Bumblyburg Science Labs after using the flying pigs as a distraction. And now, their villainous plan was in full swing! The scientists were all tied up, and Greta and Awful Alvin were pushing a giant telescope across the floor.

"How is this going to help us crack open the Mega–Safe?" asked Greta.

"Leave that to my dependable sidekick!" Awful Alvin snickered.

"Lampy? What can *he* do?" asked Greta as they placed the telescope in front of the Mega–Safe, which held the Bumblyburg Science Labs' most experimental and dangerous science projects.

Awful Alvin pointed the small end of the telescope at the safe, then put Lampy in front of the big end. "Lampy isn't just here for his pretty face and winning attitude," he told her. "He also has his own superpowers! I call it his 'Lampy Laser'!"

Alvin grabbed

Lampy's cord and prepared to plug it in. "This little lamp of mine," he sang, "I'm gonna let him shine!"

He plugged Lampy in, and Lampy's light flicked on, throwing light into the telescope. The telescope focused Lampy's light into a powerful beam, and began burning a hole in the Mega-Safe. "I'm gonna let him shine, let him shine, let him shine, let him shine!" Greta winced. Not another song and dance from Alvin!

Awful Alvin began dancing as he sang with glee. "Hide him under a bushel? NO! I'm gonna let him shine!"

Greta Von Gruesome sighed. Working with Awful Alvin was going to be about as much fun as working with a truck full of angry bees.

"Burn a hole in the Mega-Safe! I'm gonna let him shine! Burn a hole in the..."

There was a sound from above, and Awful Alvin stopped his singing. He and Greta looked up to see Dark Crow crash through the skylight in the ceiling.

"Dark Crow!" said Greta.

"That's right, dastardly doers!" crowed Dark Crow as his cape spread out like a bird, and he floated to the ground. "This crow's about to put a scare in you!"

Dark Crow whipped out his Crow-Yo (a yo-yo shaped like a crow). It zipped across the room and wrapped around Lampy's cord. Dark Crow yanked, and pulled the cord from the wall, thus shutting down the Lampy Laser.

Greta Von Gruesome fired a bolt of energy from her power gloves. But Dark Crow was too fast for her. He dodged the blast and leapt up onto the telescope, and twirled two Crow-Yo's over his head with his supersuit talons.

Then, with refined skill, Dark Crow flicked the double Crow-Yo's across the room at Greta and Awful Alvin, wrapping them up, back to back.

"Don't just stand there, Lampy," said Awful Alvin. "Get him!"

But Lampy didn't move. Alvin assumed he was waiting for the right moment.

Dark Crow ignored Lampy and leapt down from the telescope, and stood in front of the safe. "What are you criminals doing here?" he demanded. "What's in that safe that you wanted so badly?"

"We'll never tell!" said Awful Alvin.

"Oh yeah?" said Dark Crow. "Maybe I should see if Lampy will talk."

"NO!" said Awful Alvin. "Leave Lampy alone! He's villainous and all, but he'll never stand up to pressure! I'll tell you what you want to know!"

"Now we're getting somewhere," Dark Crow smirked.

CHAPTER 8
LARRYBOY LENDS A HAND

But just then, Larryboy rode up on the Larry-Unicycle, huffing and puffing mightily. **"I...AM...(PUFF, PUFF) THAT...(PUFF) HER...(PUFF, PUFF)...O!**

"Laddybuoy!" said Dark Crow. "What are you doing here? I haff things all rapid up here!"

"Not entirely," Larryboy told him as he picked up Lampy's unplugged cord. "This loose cord is a safety hazard. A good superhero always takes time to prevent accidents!"

"Laddybuoy! No!" shouted Dark Crow. But it was too late. Larryboy plugged Lampy back in, thus turning the Lampy Laser back on!

The Lampy Laser hit Dark Crow square in the chest, sending him flying backwards into the safe. He bounced off and crashed into Larryboy, sending them both sailing across the room, where they landed in a large vat of Sticky Scientific Goo (used for sticky scientific stuff).

Now that Dark Crow wasn't holding onto the Crow-Yo strings, Greta and Alvin were able to free themselves easily. "Thanks, Larryboy," said Greta. "We couldn't have escaped and continued our wicked plan without you!"

"You're welcome!" said Larryboy. "Oh…wait. You're *not* welcome!"

As Larryboy and Dark Crow sloshed around in the goo, Awful Alvin finished cutting a hole in the Mega Safe with the Lampy Laser.

When the hole was done, Awful Alvin and Greta rushed into the safe and wheeled out what looked like a laser canon. But it wasn't, it was the latest experimental wheel-mounted ray-gun invention of the Bumblyburg Science Labs!

"Now that we have this, no one will be able to stop us!" Greta said with glee. "Not even you pathetic 'super-heroes'!"

"And since no one can stop us, we will be unstoppable!" laughed Awful Alvin. "And since we are unstoppable, you can't stop us! Ha ha ha ha!"

Suddenly, he stopped laughing and got a weird look in his eye. "Ooh! I can feel another villainy dance coming on!"

"Oh give it a rest!" Greta Von Gruesome told him as she grabbed him by the arm and pulled him out the door.

CHAPTER 9

PROFESSOR FLURBLEBLUB SHARES SOME INFORMATION

Several minutes later, Larryboy and Dark Crow finally managed to pull themselves out of the vat of Sticky Scientific Goo. They untied the scientists.

"Thanks for untying us," said one of the scientists. "I'm Professor Flurbleblub, head of research here at the Labs."

"I've got Sticky Scientific Goo in my underpants," said Larryboy.

Ignoring Larryboy, Dark Crow turned to the professor. "What was that thing they stole?"

"It was one of our top-secret experiments!" replied Professor Flurbleblub.

"Eef it was top secret, how deed those villains know about it?" asked Dark Crow.

"Well, we think one of them may have been spying on us!" said Professor Flurbleblub. "Here, look at this surveillance photo." He showed Larryboy and Dark Crow a picture of Lampy wearing dark sunglasses and a fake moustache. "The thing they stole was our highly experimental Over-Easy-Egg Ray. It emits a special beam that can turn any inanimate object into over-easy eggs!"

"What's an inanimate object?" asked Larryboy.

"An inanimate object is anything that isn't alive," explained Professor Flurbleblub. "Like a rock, or a wall, or a car."

"But will they…"

Larryboy interrupted Dark Crow. "What about a cow?"

"Cows are alive," said Professor Flurbleblub. "The ray wouldn't work on a cow."

"What about a dead cow?"

"OK, a dead cow. The ray would turn a dead cow into over-easy eggs," Professor Flurbleblub conceded.

"Dastardly!" exclaimed Larryboy.

"Why would you even invent such a ray?" asked Dark Crow.

"Well…we don't always have time to make breakfast before we come to work," Professor Flurbleblub replied, sheepishly. "We're also working on a radioactive chamber to turn old hats into bagels and cream cheese."

"I like cream *and* cheese!" said Larryboy.

"So you're saying that with that ray, Greta and Awful Alvin will be able to turn anything they want eento over-easy eggs?" asked Dark Crow.

"Not anything," Larryboy corrected. "They can't turn cows into over-easy eggs."

"Unfortunately, most anything, yes," said Professor Flurbleblub. "The potential for badness just boggles the mind."

"Ees there anything you can do to stop them?" asked Dark Crow.

"Well, we did invent a special metal called 'Egganium' that is unaffected by the Over-Easy-Egg Ray," said Professor Flurbleblub. "If we didn't invent 'Egganium', we would have probably have turned the entire lab into over-easy-eggs by now! If you can give us some time, I believe we could think of a way to use that to stop the villains."

"Theese is all your fault, Laddybuoy!" said Dark Crow. "Eef you hadn't burst een on my case, those evildoers wouldn't haff that eggamatic weapon een their hands right now!"

"*Your* case?" said Larryboy. "But you're forgetting, this is *my* city!"

"Why don't you just share the case?" suggested Professor Flurbleblub. "Wouldn't God want you to share?"

"Share a case with Laddybuoy?" Dark Crow asked. "You must be joking."

"That's not a joke," said Larryboy. "Here's a joke! What do you get when you cross a water balloon with a porcupine?"

"Theese is no time for joking, Laddybuoy! Just stay out of my way! Theese case ees *mine*. I don't want to see you again until theese case ees over!"

"What about tomorrow night? That's when we have our Superhero Class together. I'll probably see you then," smiled Larryboy.

Dark Crow didn't answer, he just growled and gritted his teeth.

CHAPTER 10

NOW BOK CHOY SHARES SOME INFORMATION

The next night at Superhero Class, Larryboy and Dark Crow tried to sit as far apart as they could. But it wasn't far enough to protect them from the cold stares they received from each other.

"As we all know, sharing is very important!" said Bok Choy, the teacher of the Superhero Class. "This is something most of us learned in kindergarten."

Dark Crow glared at Larryboy. Larryboy glared back. Neither of them was really paying attention to Bok Choy.

"Why, I remember my kindergarten teacher, Miss Loochy," Bok Choy sighed wistfully. "Sometimes the bigger kids wouldn't let me use the microscopes. But Miss Loochy always said, 'OK, class! I want you to share!' I loved Miss Loochy. I thought that I would marry her when I grew up..."

Bok Choy continued as he stared off into space with a silly grin on his face.

Suddenly, a mechanical arm shot out from Dark

Crow and dangled a paper in front of Larryboy. Larryboy leaned forward and looked at the crude drawing of himself with odor lines wafting away from him. The note read, "Larryboy = Stinkiness."

Larryboy was stunned by the rude gesture! He turned and gave Dark Crow a sour look as his extension arm retracted back into his helmet.

The look on Bok Choy's face had turned sour, too. "But then, Miss Loochy went off and married the principal, *Mr. Moochy! Ooooh!* I never liked Mr. Moochy! She should have married me! After all, I became a famous superhero!!"

Larryboy fired a plunger ear that stopped short of Dark Crow who looked stunned to see the plunger hovering in front of his face. Then with a **THWOPPING** sound, a balled up paper wad shot out of the plunger and struck Dark Crow in the forehead. Dark Crow's eyes briefly crossed as he looked up at the paper wad and then leered angrily at Larryboy.

"Master Choy!" said Dark Crow. "I haff a question! What should you do eef your *brilliant* plan to apprehend multiple super-villains ees bungled by an uninvited, second-rate cucumber een purple spandex?"

"You are *not* listening to the heart of my lesson!" said Bok Choy. "To have a sharing heart doesn't just mean sharing toys or jellybeans, or even microscopes. There are many times when sharing is important. Sharing blame, sharing work, sharing responsibilities. In all these things you must also share!"

"Oh, but I have a question too," said Larryboy. "What if the town that is under your sworn protection is invaded by a super-sulker, seedless grape who thinks he's a bird!"

"Who are you calling seedless?" Dark Crow warned.

"Larryboy! Dark Crow!" said Bok Choy. "You *both* need to hear the words of my lesson and take them to heart! Heroes! Turn in your Superhero Handbooks to Section Twenty-One, Paragraph Four, Subsection Nine and Ten. 'Two are better than one because they have a good return for their work; If one falls down, his friend can help him up!"

As Bok Choy was speaking, Dark Crow fired a talon-line from his utility belt. It whipped around an overhead light and dropped down behind Larryboy, attaching to his pants.

The talon tugged and gave Larryboy a super-wedgie, lifting him momentarily out of his seat. When the cable released, Larryboy fell back to his seat with a loud *thud*.

"OOOOP!"

"When two work together, they are stronger than one," Bok Choy said sternly, looking from Larryboy to Dark Crow. "Learn today's lesson! And your many questions shall be answered."

CHAPTER 11

LARRY SCOFFS AT THE SCOOP

The next day, Larryboy's
alter ego, Larry the Janitor, reported
for work at *The Daily Bumble*. The
reporters at *The Daily Bumble* always
seemed to know everything that was going on
in Bumblyburg, so posing as a janitor was a good
way for Larryboy to pick up important information.

As Larry mopped the floor, Vicki Cucumber
strolled by. Larry thought that Vicki was the most
beautiful cucumber in all of Bumblyburg. If he could
just muster the courage to invite her to the Founder's
Day Party!

"Good morning, Vicki," he said. "What's the scoop
today?"

"Well, it looks like Larryboy tried to break up a
break-in at the Bumblyburg Science Labs last night,"
she explained as she showed him a copy of the
morning paper.

Larry looked at the front page. Larryboy's picture was on the front. But guess whose picture
was there right alongside his...Dark Crow!

239

"Looks like he had some help from Dark Crow, the dark grape from Maisefield," said Vicki. Larry frowned. The picture of Dark Crow was bigger than the picture of Larryboy!

"Why should I…um…I mean why should *Larryboy* have

to share the front page with Dark Crow? Larryboy is Bumblyburg's favorite and most handsome sworn defender! That Dark Crow is just a hero-come-lately! Why, he couldn't even carry Larryboy's..."

Just then Larry's mop rang. "What's that?" asked Vicki.

"Um, nothing."

"No, I heard something," said Vicki.

"Yeah, now I hear it too," Larry agreed. "I think it's the sound of a toilet about to overflow. I better go take care of it, since I am the janitor and all."

"Ok. I'm on my way to the museum for a photo shoot, anyway. See you later, Larryboy!" Vicki called after him. But Larryboy was already gone.

Larry hopped into the janitor closet. He knew that the beeping was coming from his mop. Archie had installed a communicator in Larry's mop to contact him when there was a Larryboy emergency. But Larryboy really needed to talk to Archie about the beeping. Sometimes, it could be *really* embarrassing.

Larry threw the mop over his head, thus activating the video screen that linked him to Archie in the Larrycave. "Master Larry, I have some terrible news," said Archie. "Awful Alvin, Greta Von Gruesome, and Lampy have just been spotted outside of the Bumblyburg Museum of History and Old Stuff."

"I bet they're there to check out the mummy exhibit," said Larryboy. "I've been meaning to go see it myself!"

"Not likely. I suspect that they have nothing but mischief on their warped minds! This looks like a job for Larryboy!"

CHAPTER 12

TWO PHARAOHS AND A QUEEN

The Bumblyburg Museum of History and Old Stuff contained several priceless old things made of gold and jewels. As a result, every super-villain worth their wicked cackle wanted to break in and steal the Old Stuff.

But the walls of the museum were protected with reinforced steel and concrete. No super-villain had ever broken in.

That was about to change.

Awful Alvin hovered outside the museum walls on his hovering platform. It was one of the things that his awful mind had invented. It was handy to float around town and to hover above someone's head if he wanted to dump a bucket of soapy water on them. But now, he was using it for something different. He had hooked the Over-Easy-Egg Ray to the platform, and was hovering just outside the Museum of History and Old Stuff with Greta and Lampy onboard as well.

"HA HA HA," laughed Awful Alvin. "Mere

walls can't keep us out now that we have the power of the Over-Easy-Egg Ray!

"**FIRE!**" commanded Greta.

"Would it kill you to say, 'please'?" asked Awful Alvin.

Inside the museum, Mrs. Celery was leading her class through the mummy exhibit just as Vicki arrived to take pictures.

Junior posed beside a mummy-wrapped asparagus and said, "Take this shot! My headline can be, 'Me and My Mummy!'"

Bob just grumbled. "That's fine for a school newspaper, Junior. But it's not the kind of story that sells in Bumblyburg. I wish something exciting would happen around here."

"And here we have the royal clothing of Pharaoh Edward Potatothep of Ancient Egypt," Mrs. Celery said as she led the group over to a small sphinx, that was just about her height. "And this was the Pharaoh's sphinx."

"Did you say the Pharaoh stinks?" asked Junior Asparagus.

"No, no! The Pharaoh's sphinx!"

But before Mrs. Celery had a chance to fully explain, the room was filled with a **WOBBLE-WOBBLE** sort of sound.

"What is that noise?" asked Mrs. Celery.

A moment later, her question was answered, as the wall of the museum turned to over-easy eggs right before their very eyes, and fell down on top of her and her students.

"Yuck! Over-easy eggs!" said one of the students.

Another student shrugged and took a bite. "Better than cafeteria lunch."

Awful Alvin, Greta, and Lampy floated into the room on the floating platform.

"It's Awful Alvin and Greta Von Gruesome!" shouted Mrs. Celery as she wiped the eggs from her eyes. "Run children! Run!"

The children just stood and stared at her. "Um, I mean, line up and file out in an orderly fashion, please," she clarified. "But do it quickly!" And the children did just that. They were very good little students.

"**HA HA HA HA HA!**" laughed Awful Alvin, who was neither good nor little. "Finally, the forbidden treasures of the Bumblyburg Museum shall be mine! All mine! All miney-meanie-miney-mo-mine!"

"What do you mean 'all yours'?" said Greta. "I get my share, too!"

"Of course, of course," said Awful Alvin as he grabbed the royal headdress of Pharaoh Potatophep and placed it on his own head. "Look at me! I'm a Pharaoh! Pharaoh Alvin!" he gloated as he placed another headdress on Lampy. "Look at us! Two Pharaohs out on the town! Lookin' sharp! Check us out, the coolest Pharaohs you ever will meet! Oh yeah!" Awful Alvin grabbed Lampy and strutted around the museum floor.

Using some velvet rope from one of the exhibits, Greta and Alvin tied up Bob, Vicki, and Junior.

"You'll never get away with this! Larryboy will stop you!" Vicki said as she glared at the menacing duo.

"Hey, Lampy!" said Alvin. "I've got an idea! Let's give ourselves a big Pharaoh cheer!" He set Lampy down and began waving his arms wildly like a cheerleader. **"GIMME AN 'F'... 'F!' GIMME AN 'A'... 'A!' GIMME AN 'R'... 'R!' GIMME AN 'O'... 'O!' GIMME A 'W'... 'W!' WHAT DOES IT SPELL?"** he called out.

But no one said anything.

"Lampy, what does is spell?"

Lampy didn't say anything.

"It spells FAROW!" said Awful Alvin. "Gooo Farows!"

"That's not how you spell Pharaoh!" said Vicki.

"You're just jealous that you don't get to be in our Farow Club!" said Alvin as he looked to Lampy for agreement. "Oh, Lampy, doesn't this villainy just make you feel like..."

Greta whirled around, cutting Alvin off, "One more dance step and I'll serve you on toast with a side of bacon!"

"Now this is what I call news!" said Bob, as he tried to

wiggle free from the ropes that kept him bound.

"If I could get free, I could snap a front page photo of the villains!" Vicki added.

Greta hopped over to the other side of the museum and used her power gloves to blast through the protective glass surrounding Queen Loopy Goop the Fourth's royal crown. She placed the crown on her head. "All shall bow! Bow before your queen!" she said, addressing her imaginary subjects. She put on the queen's robes, grabbed the queen's royal scepter, and sat in the queen's royal throne. "Now bring the queen some honey-roasted peanuts! And somebody scratch my back in that spot I can never reach! Your queen commands it!"

Before long, all three of them were dressed from top to bottom in the most expensive royal clothing in all history. They started loading all kinds of gold and jewels on Alvin's floating platform to take with them when they left. Of course, both Alvin and Greta were planning to trick each other and keep all the riches for themselves, but for now, they were just having too much fun stealing stuff to think about that!

Greta approached a mummy's tomb, giddy with excitement. "I wonder what's in here!" she cackled. "Probably filled with diamonds and rubies...or maybe a fondue set. I love fondue!"

Greta used the queen's scepter to pry the tomb open. But when she opened it, she saw no jewels. Instead, all she heard was...

"CA-CAW!"

CHAPTER 13

OVER-EASY-EGG RAY UNLEASHED!

"Prepare to eat crow-
bar!" said Dark Crow as he whipped
out his crow-bar, preparing to ensnare
the villains once again. "I knew you two
couldn't resist trying to rob the museum!"
But Greta was too quick for him this time
and knocked the crowbar away with the scepter.
"Prepare to bow before your queen, peasant!"
said Greta as she swung the scepter at Dark Crow.
Just then, the Larrymobile drove in through the
over-easy-egg hole in the wall. **"I AM THAT HERO!"**
Larryboy exclaimed as he leapt from his supercar.
"Laddybuoy!" said Dark Crow. "I thought I told you
to stay out of theese!"
"You can't just claim a case in my city and...
look out!"
Larryboy's warning came just in time. Dark Crow
blocked another blow from Greta's scepter with the
crowbar. But he was off balance, and tripped,
causing him to roll across the room and crash into
a large pillar. The pillar began to tip and fell
right toward Bob, Vicki, and Junior!

"Larryboy! Help!" cried Vicki.

Larryboy whirled around and shot a plunger ear which attached to Bob's forehead. The rope went taut and Larryboy pulled the tied-up trio out from under the pillar just seconds before the pillar crashed to floor.

"Let's get out of here!" Bob said to Junior as they quickly hopped out the hole in the over-easy wall.

Vicki spun out of the velvet ropes and twirled right into Larryboy's......arms?

"Vicki, I want to ask you something about the Founder's Day Party," Larryboy said as the words tumbled out before he even knew he'd said them.

"Oh Larryboy! What is it?" she asked, looking dreamily into his eyes.

"Um…this year…are they going to have refreshments like hot fudge sundaes at the party?" he said with a somewhat squeaky voice.

"Did you say, party? I was born to party!" Dark Crow chimed in as Spanish music surrounded him.

Larryboy turned to face Dark Crow. "Hey! Ya mind?"

"Yes, I *do* mind, Laddybuoy! I had things under control here before you arrived!" said Dark Crow.

"Did not!" said Larryboy.

"Did too!"

"Did not with lemons on top!"

"Sorry to interrupt your strategic superhero planning session," said a voice from above them. They both looked up to see Awful Alvin and Lampy looking down at them from the floating platform. The Over-Easy-Egg Ray was pointed right at them. "I just thought you might like to be made aware that you're about to be the victims of a concentrated blast of pure villainy!"

"We know all about your Over-Easy-Egg Ray!" said Dark Crow. "It can't hurt us!"

"Yeah," agreed Larryboy. "We're not a laminated object!"

"In*animate* object!" corrected Dark Crow.

"That's what I said," said Larryboy.

"No, it wasn't."

"Besides, we're not wooden cows!" Larryboy said, finishing the argument.

"You're right," interrupted Alvin, who was getting tired of the heroes always talking when he wanted to taunt and mock them. "It won't work on you. But I think it will

work quite well on your supersuits!"

Larryboy and Dark Crow's eyes went wide. Their super crime-fighting costumes!

OH NO!

WOBBLE-WOBBLE! Awful Alvin zapped them. Larryboy and Dark Crow looked at one another.

"Better quiche your super-costumes goodbye!" Greta cackled.

"Um....you're covered in eggs," said Larryboy.

"So are you," Dark Crow pointed out.

Awful Alvin and Greta laughed.

"You won't get away with this!" said Larryboy. He turned his head to fire his plunger ear, but the result was a lump of eggs that fell off the side of his head. Even his plungers had been turned to eggs!

"Sorry, Larryboy!" said Greta. "We *will* get away with it! We will get away with all the loot we can carry! We're even taking the Pharaoh's sphinx!"

"Did you say the Pharaoh stinks?" asked Larryboy.

"No! The Pharaoh's sphinx!"

"I really don't think that's what you said," Larryboy told her.

"That sphinx is property of honest and good citizens!" said Dark Crow. "I'll stop you, costume or no costume!" He leapt toward Green Greta, but she blasted him with her power gloves, sending him rolling back into the mummy's tomb. Then Greta hopped back up onto the floating platform, and prepared to exit.

"See you later, super zeroes," said Awful Alvin. "Maybe you better run home to your mummy! Ha ha ha! Get it? Mummy?"

The villains swooped past Vicki who had just bent over to pick up her camera. Seeing Vicki gave Alvin another awful idea. He reached over and scooped her onto the platform.

"You two super-losers had better let us go about our villainous villainy or the newspaper gal gets egged!"

"LARRYBOY! HEEEEELLLLPPP!" Vicki screamed as the villains flew out the museum with Vicki on board.

CHAPTER 14

A COSTUME PARTY

Once the villains left, Larryboy and Dark Crow realized they couldn't just go around trying to catch super-villains wearing nothing but over-easy eggs. They had to wipe the egg off their faces and get back to work!

Fortunately, Larryboy found a bag of clothes in a dumpster in the alley behind the Museum. *Unfor*tunately, the bag of clothes contained nothing but fuzzy pajamas.

Larryboy chose fuzzy yellow pj's with teddy bears, while Dark Crow chose fuzzy green pj's with race cars. It was the best they could do.

Then Larryboy had an idea that they should also wear paper bags over their heads to protect their secret identities. Dark Crow thought this was a good idea, but he did suggest that they cut eye-holes in the bags so they could see. Larryboy reluctantly agreed.

Once they had changed into their new "costumes",

Larryboy hopped out from behind a dumpster. "How do I look?" he asked.

"You look ridiculous," said Dark Crow.

"So do you," said Larryboy.

They were both right.

But Larryboy brightened when he found an old plunger in the dumpster. He carefully tied it to his head. "This will help everyone know that it's me…Larryboy."

"I don't know about theese new costumes," said Dark Crow. "They don't exactly strike fear into the hearts of evildoers everywhere. Maybe we should go home and get

our spare costumes."

"You can go home if you want," said Larryboy. "But Greta and Awful Alvin have Vicki! I have no time to be concerned about fashion!"

Dark Crow agreed. (He wasn't about to let Larryboy capture the villains by himself and take all the credit.) They decided they should return to the Bumblyburg Science Labs. Maybe Professor Flurbleblub and the other scientists had come up with a way to defeat the Over-Easy-Egg Ray.

CHAPTER 15

THE BUNNY-BOT 3000

Larryboy and Dark Crow made their way over to the Science Labs. Once Professor Flurbleblub and the other scientists stopped laughing at their new costumes, they took the heroes down to the high-security sub-basement of the labs and stood them in front of a large metal door.

"Have you figured out a way to stop the Over-Easy-Egg Ray?" asked Larryboy.

"We hope so," said Professor Flurbleblub. "We took the Egganium and used it to create...this!"

He pressed a button, and the large metal door slid open to reveal...a giant metal bunny.

"You created a mega-bunny?" asked Dark Crow.

"It's the ultimate Over-Easy-Egg Fighting robot suit!" said Professor Flurbleblub. "The Bunny-Bot 3000! You get inside and control the robot's movements."

"But, why would you shape it like a bunny?" asked Larryboy.

"Well...we think bunnies are real cute,"

Professor Flurbleblub answered sheepishly. "There's just one problem. We only had enough Eggananium to make one Bunny-Bot. You'll have to share."

"Share?" asked a stunned Dark Crow. "No-hip-hopping-bunny-trailing-way! Theese is *my* case!"

"But it's *my* city!" said Larryboy.

"You know, you are right, Laddybuoy. By the way, your shoe's untied!" chuckled Dark Crow.

Larryboy looked down. "What? I'm not wearing any shoes. I don't even have any feet!"

"I know," said Dark Crow. But while Larryboy was looking for his shoes, Dark Crow had slipped into the Bunny-Bot. "Adios, Jammie-boy. Vicki, have no fear, de Dark Crow is coming to safe you!"

"Hey! No fair!" said Larryboy.

The rocket thrusters in the Bunny-Bot's feet fired up, and Dark Crow lifted off.

"You're not leaving without me!" called Larryboy. He jumped toward the robot with a big **KER-PLOK!** As he attached himself with the plunger that was tied to his head, the ceiling opened up and the Bunny-Bot's rocket thrusters roared to life. The scientists watched as they blasted through the roof.

"WHOOOOOOAAAAH!" said Larryboy.

CHAPTER 16

SHIMMYING WITH BADNESS

At that moment in downtown Bumblyburg, just beneath *The Daily Bumble* building, Mayor Flapjack's car was being turned into a big lump of gooey eggs. Moments later, a traffic light was turned into eggs. A telephone pole, a fountain, and a kissing booth, all turned to over-easy eggs.

Awful Alvin, Greta Von Gruesome, and Lampy were floating around town, randomly turning things into eggs. Just because they could. And just because they were bad.

"Sometimes, I simply love being bad!" said Awful Alvin. "And this is one of those times! My badness is like a tickle in my tummy that makes me want to shake and shimmy. Shimmy with badness! Shimmy with me Lampy!"

But just as Awful Alvin began to shimmy, there was a roar overhead. The villains looked up and saw something flying through the sky.

"Look, up in the sky!" said Greta.

"It's a weather balloon."

"It's a metallic flying fish!" thought Awful Alvin.

The Bunny-Bot 3000 zoomed toward the dastardly duo, with Larryboy still attached.

"WHHHOOOOOAAAAAA!" said Larryboy.

"It's a cucumber wearing pajamas attached to a bunny-shaped robot," said Greta.

"It's Larryboy!" exclaimed Vicki.

The Bunny-Bot landed in front of the super-villains who were hovering a few feet off the ground. "Halt, you villains!" said Dark Crow from inside the bunny suit. "Your days of foul deeds are over!"

"Don't you mean over-*easy*?" said Greta.

She fired the Over-Easy-Egg Ray at the Bunny-Bot, fully expecting it to turn to eggs. But the Egganium stood firm and did not turn to egg. It remained distinctly un-egg-like!

"What!?" said Awful Alvin. "How can this be?"

"Looks like you're headed to prison to do some hard-*boiled* time!" boasted Dark Crow.

The Bunny-Bot's arms extended to the villains, and reached out to grab them with its metal claws.

Just then Larryboy hopped out from behind the robot in his pj's and paper bag. "Dark Crow! It's my turn to use the Bunny-Bot!" he cried.

"No way!" said Dark Crow.

"You got to fly it here!"

"That doesn't count!"

While the two heroes were arguing, Awful Alvin created another awful plan. He might not be able to turn the Bunny-Bot into eggs, but there was more than one way to defeat a super-hero.

Awful Alvin pointed the Over-Easy-Egg Ray up at the roof of *The Daily Bumble* building, and fired. **WOBBLE-WOBBLE!** The statue of a giant bumble bee atop the building turned to eggs and slid from the roof, falling to the street below.

"Of course it counts!" said Larryboy. "So now it's my tur..."

SPLAT!

Larryboy, Dark Crow, and the Bunny-Bot were trapped beneath two tons of over-easy eggs.

CHAPTER 17

A SKILLET SITUATION

When Larryboy and Dark Crow awoke, they were in Awful Alvin's lair. This is a bad place to be at any time. For one thing, this is where Awful Alvin usually is. For another thing, it smells really bad.

But as if being in Awful Alvin's lair wasn't bad enough, Larryboy, Dark Crow, and Vicki all found themselves tied to the Pharaoh's sphinx. And if *that* wasn't bad enough, the sphinx was suspended from the ceiling. But wait, it gets worse! The sphinx was suspended above a giant skillet that was being heated by the Lampy Laser, while the Bunny-Bot stood uselessly in the corner. And to top it all off, Greta Von Gruesome and Awful Alvin (who were still wearing their stolen finery from the museum) had the Over-Easy-Egg Ray pointed right at them!

"Good morning, eggy heads!" said Greta.

"What's the meaning of theese?" demanded Dark Crow.

"Don't worry, Vicki. I'll get us out of this," Larryboy whispered.

"You? Ha!" Dark Crow...well, he crowed. "I

once again laugh een your vesh-a-table face. Only a fruit like me can safe us now!"

"Oh, that's quite unlikely!" said Awful Alvin. "You see, my plan is almost villainously simple!"

"With just a flick of the switch, the Over-Easy-Egg Ray turns that sphinx into a big glob of eggs," explained Greta. "Those eggs will plop down into the skillet. And since you're tied to the sphinx, you're about to become the world's biggest superhero and Vicki omelet!"

"I wanted to make a superhero quiche," said Awful Alvin. "But Greta said we didn't have a flaky enough crust for you two flakes!"

"Hokay, see how you mess up my plans! Make me wear paper bags over my head. My anger for you eese enraging largely, as we speak, my friend," Dark Crow said as he glowered at Larryboy.

"What about the way you try to take over my superhero territory? AND the girl I'm inviting to the Founder's Day Party!"

Vicki's eyes widened and she smiled. But before she could speak, Dark Crow interrupted.

"Vicki, tell him that...de Dark Crow ees your favorite!" he said with a hop as Spanish music began to play...from somewhere.

"Both of you stop it! Look!" Vicki cried.

Greta and Alvin had approached the Egg Ray.

"Quiet, you two!" demanded Greta. "I think it's time for things to get cookin'!"

They were ready to seal the doom of the troubled trio forever.

CHAPTER 18

LARRYBOY AND DARK CROW REALIZE SOMETHING

"And now, I will flip the switch and say goodbye forever!" said Greta.

"You?" challenged Awful Alvin. "I, Awful Alvin, the most villainous mind of our time should be allowed to finish them off!"

"Nay!" said Greta. "I've waited too long for this moment to let a smelly little onion flip the switch!"

"Such an awful deed as this should only be done by the most awful villain! And I, Awful Alvin, could out-awful you with one root behind my back!"

"Don't make me zap you with my power gloves!" warned Greta.

By this time, Larryboy and Dark Crow had stopped their own arguing to listen to the bickering bad guys.

"You know," Larryboy pointed out, "if they'd just quit arguing, they could have finished us off by now."

"How foolish they are!" said Dark Crow. "Eef they would simply share the task, they could haff feen-ished us off by now."

"Yeah! They'd both get what they wanted if they'd work together."

Suddenly, at the mere mention of the words "share and work together", both Larryboy and Dark Crow were reminded of the lesson that Bok Choy had been trying to teach them in superhero class. They remembered him saying, "When two work together, they are stronger than one."

"Laddybuoy," said Dark Crow. "I just realized something. We haff forgotten Master Choy's lesson. We should haff been sharing!"

"Yeah, sharing the responsibilities of catching the villains, and working together to capture them!" agreed Larryboy.

"Just like we should haff shared the blame when things went wrong."

"And the Bunny-bot suit."

"And our super-abilities," said Dark Crow. "Eef we had shared those things and worked together, we would haff caught the villains by now!"

"God likes it when we work together," Vicki added, trying to encourage her superheroes.

"Well, maybe it's not too late," said Larryboy. "If we share our abilities now, we might still have a chance of getting out of this mess! Let's work together!"

"Side by side, my friend!" agreed Dark Crow.

CHAPTER 19

SUCCESSFUL SHARING

"OK, OK!" said Awful Alvin. "Why don't we vote on who gets to flip the switch?"

"Lampy's vote doesn't count," said Greta.

"Of course it counts! He's heating the skillet!"

"Guys! I think if we can bump the telescope just right, we might have a chance. What do you think?" Vicki asked.

Larryboy and Dark Crow shot each other a look and then turned back to Vicki.

"You know, you're pretty sharp for someone who's never been to a superhero class!" Larryboy told her.

As the villains continued to argue about who would get to flip the switch, Larryboy and Dark Crow worked together to swing the sphinx back and forth.

They kept working together, swinging the sphinx farther and farther until…

bump! They hit the telescope, causing it to spin around.

The focused light from Lampy shot across the room, hitting the Egganium coated Bunny-Bot which reflected the light across the room. The light then cut the rope that held the sphinx to the ceiling!

Since the sphinx was swinging back and forth, it flew away from the skillet, and landed on the hard floor. The sphinx shattered and the heroes were able to slip out of their bonds. They were free!

"Great shot, Laddybuoy!" said Dark Crow.

"You too!" said Larryboy. "We did it together!"

Unfortunately, the shattering of the sphinx on the floor was noisy enough to draw the attention of Greta and Awful Alvin. "They've escaped!" shrieked Greta.

"Get them!" yelled Alvin.

Larryboy and Dark Crow rushed to the Bunny-Bot as

the villains pushed each other out of the way in an
attempt to get to the Over-Easy-Egg Ray.

"Who's turn is it?" asked Larryboy as they reached the
Bunny-Bot.

"Eet's your turn, Laddybuoy," said Dark Crow. "After all I
deed get to fly it here. So get inside while I draw their fire."

Dark Crow jumped out from behind the Bunny-Bot.
"Hey! Over here! Nya-nya nya-nya blah-blah!"

"No one 'nya-nya's' Greta Von Gruesome!"

WOBBLE-WOBBLE! She fired the Over-Easy-Egg Ray at
Dark Crow, but he was able to jump out of the way.

While Greta was busy with Dark Crow, Larryboy
jumped inside the Bunny-Bot and it blinked to life.

Dark Crow continued hopping around, trying to distract
Greta from what Larryboy was doing. "Nya-nya!" But he

wasn't watching where he was going and ran into a wall. "Nya-nya, nya…oof!" He fell over and was trapped against the wall.

"Now I've got you!" said Greta. "Prepare for your precious pj's to become poultry progeny!"

"Poultry what?" asked Dark Crow.

"I said…oh never mind!" Greta fired the ray again. **WOBBLE-WOBBLE.**

But at the last instant, the Bunny-Bot, piloted by Larryboy, stepped in the way of the Over-Easy-Egg Ray and shielded Dark Crow. "Prepare to get 'beaten' villains!"

The hands of the Bunny-Bot transformed into eggbeaters which spun with a **WHIRRRRR!** Larryboy brought the eggbeater arms down on the Over-Easy-Egg Ray, scrambling it to pieces once and for all.

"That's my cucumber!" cheered Vicki.

"Drat," said Greta.

"Way to go, Laddybuoy!" said Dark Crow.

But Awful Alvin had managed to run for cover.

"We're not defeated yet!" sneered Awful Alvin! "Let's see if your robot is Lampy-Laser proof, too!"

Alvin fired the Lampy Laser at the Bunny-Bot, cutting through the robot's leg. (As it turns out, Egganium is very resistant to Over-Easy-Egg Rays, but otherwise, it's pretty worthless.) The Bunny-Bot fell to the floor.

"Yikes!" said Larryboy. "Where's the eject button? Shouldn't there be an eject button!"

"Get him, Lampy!" Alvin shouted. "You may have destroyed my Over-Easy-Egg Ray, but I can still destroy you!"

But before he could get off another shot, Dark Crow whipped his crow-yo out from his jammies and ensnared Lampy's cord. With one big yank, the cord was ripped from the wall. Then the crow-yo whipped back around the awful villains, trapping them tightly together.

Lampy spun, wiggled, and shook, causing all of them to topple over with a loud crash! Dark Crow swung one of his talon-lines and landed beside the bunny as Larryboy hopped out.

"Great working weeth you, pardner!" he said.

"Look! Greta is running for the door!" Vicki shrieked.

Larryboy turned to Dark Crow and together they were able to shoot Larryboy's makeshift plunger ear at the villian. Greta was encircled with a big **WHHOOOSH,** but she ducked just in time. Whirling toward the door, she taunted the superheroes as she hopped away. "Sorry, boys, you missed!"

Continuing to work together, the superheros once again shot Larryboy's improvised plunger and Dark Crow's crow-yo at the door and pulled. It forced Greta backward into a large vat of scientific goo.

"Sorry, evildoers," said Larryboy. "This time, things didn't turn out sunny-side up!"

CHAPTER 20

TRUTH AND SHARE

Later, with Greta Von Gruesome, Awful Alvin, and Lampy safely in jail, Larryboy and Dark Crow went back to the Bumblyburg Science Labs to return the telescope the villains had stolen. (But not before taking a moment to change into their spare costumes.)

Bob and Junior stood nearby as Vicki flashed pictures of the momentous event.

"Thank you," said Professor Flurbleblub. "This telescope is very important to us."

"Do you use it to look at faraway galaxies?" asked Larryboy?

"Sometimes," said Professor Flurbleblub. "Mostly we use it to help look for our lost car keys."

"Well, I have to share the credit with Dark Crow," Larryboy pointed out. "I couldn't have done it without him."

"And I couldn't have done eet without Laddybuoy. He taught me why sharing ees important...even for a superhero."

"Because when two people work together, they are more powerful than either one of them is alone!" Larryboy said, echoing the words of his superhero teacher.

"Oh, I can see the headline, now," Bob said. "'Teamwork Tosses Bad Guys' Salad!' Or maybe, 'United We Stand, Divided We Get Egg On Our Faces!' Or, or...."

As Bob decided which headline was best, Vicki made her way over to talk to her favorite superhero. "Was there something you wanted to ask me about Founder's Day, Larryboy?"

"Gosh. Founder's Day....Umm..." he said, pondering Vicki's words as he looked toward the sky. "Wow, drawing blanks here."

"Didn't you want to ask me to the Founder's Day Party, Larry?"

"OOOOOO.....RRRRRRIIIIGHT," Larryboy stuttered.

"I'd love to go with you!"

"Wow! Really?" Larryboy said as they hopped out of the laboratory with Dark Crow close behind them.

"Maybe we could have a nice dinner together, first," Vicki suggested.

"Hey, Laddybuoy! We're a team, are we not?" Dark Crow called after them.

Vicki and Larryboy stopped and smiled as Dark Crow caught up to them.

"We must do *everything* together now. I will show you how to dance because I yem – de Dark Crow!" he said, striking a pose as Spanish music began to play.

"Where does that music come from?" Larryboy asked as they all hopped off together.

"I like you so much, Laddybuoy! No matter what anybody

else says about you. You know, I haff a very talented chore-ographer you should meet. She does all my music," Dark Crow told him. "Een fact, I am looking for a stunt double. Think about it, Laddybuoy. I mean getting egged like we did, ees not the way we should be seen by our public. No, no no. We are superheroes, you and me....."

"Hey! Larryboy and Dark Crow didn't stay to see our latest experiment," said Professor Flurbleblub. "And I think they would have been so impressed. After all, no one else has ever thought of inventing a set of wings that will help pigs fly!"

Life was never easy for a superhero.

THE END

We want to hear from you. Please send your comments about this book to us in care of zreview@zondervan.com. Thank you.

ZONDERVAN.com/
AUTHORTRACKER
follow your favorite authors